BEYOND THE PALE

Short Stories By

M.V. Montgomery

Winter Goose Publishing

Winter Goose Publishing
2701 Del Paso Road, 130-92
Sacramento, CA 95835

www.wintergoosepublishing.com
Contact Information: info@wintergoosepublishing.com

Beyond the Pale

COPYRIGHT © 2013 by M.V. Montgomery

First Edition, May 2013

ISBN: 978-0-9889049-8-9

Cover Art by Winter Goose Publishing
Photograph by Paul Nine-O
Typeset by Michelle Lovi

Published in the United States of America

To Molly,
who usually gets me

CONTENTS

I

BEYOND THE PALE

1

In all the trades I had read about a new production called *Track of the Vampire*, later retitled simply *The Vampire*, but confess I had tuned the matter out.

Two of my least favorite genres, certainly: the already far-overdone vampire pic combined with a reality-show premise. Something this time about a search to find an "authentic" vampire to fill the top of the bill by scouring Old World countries where such a species might persist—if one had ever existed at all.

I was content to skip over this news item at the time and heard no more buzz about the project for several months.

Then a full page ad appeared, announcing a "major discovery" that would rock the world. A new creative team had been deployed including my producer friend Gideon Smith and a very high-profile director whose name has since been erased from the project, and which I am not at liberty to disclose.

For a brief while, *The Vampire* became the talk of the tabloids, and network entertainment programs announced forthcoming "sneak peeks" providing thrills like nothing the viewer had ever seen.

Then just as suddenly, a one-sentence press release announced the production had been shut down.

No one was talking.

Now curious, I texted Gideon without revealing my true motives. Only mentioned that it would be nice to get together for lunch with my old film school roommate.

I had single-handedly kept Gideon alive in the early '80s while most of his parent-wired money was spent on alcohol and drugs. Over the years, karma had nicely returned the serve by turning him into my favorite unnamed source in the industry.

2

Uncharacteristically, Gideon wasn't very talkative on the day we met. As we were shown to our booth, he even looked genuinely haunted (for someone with a permanent tan).

"Just forget about it," he said. "I'm under strict orders to keep things quiet."

So he had guessed my purpose, after all.

"Sure I can forget," I reminded him, "just the way you've forgotten those trips to the hospital in the middle of the night to have your sizable stomach pumped, or the time I had to bail you out for drunk and disorderly."

"M.V., please, don't make me."

I knew not only would Gideon tell me, but he actually wanted and needed to talk to someone. So I said nothing.

"You promise anonymity?"

"Gideon, please."

"Promise?"

Gideon. Please.

3

In that way, I got the story, or the first part of it anyway.

Gideon's crew arrived on location in mid-October in Slovenia, where the original small production had come to a halt until the heavy artillery could be called in.

I assumed this was because the search for a vampire, having proved futile, necessitated a serious upgrade in creative personnel?

"No," Gideon retorted. "The search was not a bust. We found ourselves a genuine *pijavica!*"

"What?"

"It's the local word for a blood-sucking vampire."

"Skip the linguistics, man."

"The location scouts found him in a bar, flush-faced with what they naturally assumed was drink. He was an old guy singing and carrying on. He had begun his second life drinking animal blood, and now was reverting back to that food like a senior on mush.

"Not exactly the romantic male lead the studio had envisioned, yet this guy was very real. Plied with fresh meat, he revived a little and began to show off his powers."

"I see," I said. (I didn't believe a word of this.)

"The whole concept was jeopardized. The original plan was to shoot some cheesy *Interview with the Vampire* stuff, some noir kinds of scenes, then maybe fix the guy up with Reese Witherspoon."

I groaned. Such is Hollywood.

"But this guy was a chatterbox, a Joe Pesci-type character who complained nonstop about his family. You know what? He was actually his own brother's son. Kind of a twisted family tree! This guy wasn't shy about talking about killing his brother and his mother, too. This was dark stuff, M.V. That's what first interested Wern—"

He cut himself off before he finished speaking the famous director's name.

My eyebrow raised to half-mast.

"When I got there, it was partly for damage control, you know, to shut this guy up. Have some gravitas, for God's sake!

"The thing was, the more the old guy found an audience, the more he warmed up to the room, and the better and fresher blood he demanded.

"One day it had to be a goat, the next day a newborn bull, and soon he was sucking on human plasma and having the whole crew line up for transfusions.

"It was crazy, but kind of exciting. The more this guy drank, the more his vitality spiked. You know, he even had more than one of the production assistants offering themselves up to him alfresco."

One thing I should interrupt here to tell you about Gideon. His morals may have been the pits, but I'd never known the guy to lie to your face. If anything, when we were students I wished he would've practiced a little more stealth. So by this point, I was listening.

It was then I remembered the production had broken off suddenly. I thought I could guess the reason for that.

"It must have been like Max von Schreck in *Nosferatu* all over again," I offered, "with an allegedly real vampire becoming rabid and attacking the crew."

I continued associating while we locked into our entrée selections. The waiter was speaking something into my ear about alligator frittatas. The décor surrounding us was faux jungle, framing our booth in palm fronds.

Gideon sat back in his seat, easing the pressure on his belly. Absently, he began playing with the menu options on his phone.

What, was he trying to bail on me?

Not a chance. He saw me giving him the stink eye.

"Well, the networks were quietly being lined up. Not just the regulars, you know; we had *60 Minutes* and *Animal Planet* on standby.

"By this point, we had our lusty *pijavican* on a tight leash. He had been read the riot act until he understood—any violence, the tap is closed!

"I tell you, this guy was like, entering his second childhood. It probably didn't help that the veins of some of the production crew were full of pharmaceuticals."

"No," he added, "the decision to shut down came straight from the studio heads."

"We'd been overnighting the rushes to LA immediately, in sealed canisters. Tight security, you know. Most of our sets were closed to begin with, but we didn't want anyone walking into the dailies and getting a preview of our star.

"And that, in the end, was the problem."

I confessed I didn't understand.

"Here, I'd better show you," Gideon said, firing up his iPhone.

We had to wait a minute until he found the file he was looking for.

He pointed the tiny screen across the table at me.

In the clip, I saw the famous director's face as he began his narration about the vampire's supernatural ability to leap and flit through the forest world.

Then the handheld camera panned shakily to a nearby lane of old linden trees.

It held for a long time on a few that looked to be nearly a hundred feet tall.

It was a misty day—well-chosen, I suppose, for creating a somber, supernatural mood—if such was the intent. But there is only so long one cares to look at trees.

Another minute of this passed.

"I see nothing," I complained to Gideon.

"Exactly," he replied.

THE HEART OF THE MATTER

1

I have a guilty confession to make. The opening scene of director Victor Tata's debut film *Hellish Picnic* (1986; original title, *Infernal Town*) comprises a sequence of images which I have always unduly admired.

The scene is set at a campground much like any other, on a fine day, with clouds scudding across the sky. We open on forested hillside looking down upon a line of picnic tables winding down to a pavilion. All is peaceful. Then, out of somewhere in the deep background, an evil cloud is unleashed.

The following sequence impresses the viewer as simultaneously the product of out-of-control chaos and ingenious choreography.

The camera tilts down from a high, slightly askew angle, juddering as it catches random townspeople attempting to escape the spreading darkness, stumbling, and becoming possessed. The whole scene collapses in upon itself in one smooth wave as more and more picnickers fall under the soul-sucking influence, change countenance from wholesome to horrible, and commence tearing each other apart. Even nature itself seems complicit in the carnage, as the sun is briefly occluded.

In one unforgettable moment, a middle-aged man lunges toward the camera and sinks into a pool of darkness. His face, half-framed in natural light, disappears briefly from view. It reappears a few beats later, shrouded in shadow. That look of desperate panic now replaced by something else—something satanic.

You might think you are watching a battlefield scene shot by Jean Renoir, not someone whose name would later become synonymous with B-pictures.

True, that kind of artistic gap between a young director's first film and his later, big-budgeted work is not unheard of. And yet the opening sequence in *Hellish Picnic* is arguably what made Tata's whole career, for I was not the only reviewer to have celebrated it.

After attracting some minor film festival buzz, the film was picked up by a studio subsidiary and did above-average box office, helping to spawn the rest of the *Hellish* franchise.

Most entries in this series are now utterly forgettable: *Hellish Halloween* (1988), *Hellish Job* (1989), *Hellish Weekend* (1990), *Hellish Afternoon* (1993), and the truly misbegotten farce *Hellish Vacation* (1998). Studio products all, and loaded up with special effects like a Dagwood sandwich. And all, for the most part, lacking the spontaneity of the original (though *Hellish Afternoon* still has its defenders).

2

I encountered Vic Tata himself not long ago at the Whole Foods Market. I reintroduced myself (we had met at an awards ceremony in 1991, but no chance he remembered me). He had an advanced case of Parkinson's and could no longer walk, so I helped his personal assistant lift him into a chair and bought Vic a fresh-squeezed juice.

We got to talking a bit about the old days. It was inevitable, I suppose, that the scene which had once crept into my own nightmares would emerge as a topic of conversation.

I expressed my appreciation anew for *Hellish Picnic* and asked Vic how in the world he had gotten the timing of that initial sequence just right.

He surprised me by refusing to accept any praise. "It was the hand of God," he just commented, elliptically.

The irony of the remark amused me, given the satanic content of all Tata movies.

"I never cared much for devils!" Vic sputtered. "Evil, despicable creatures!"

Then he abruptly shifted tone—adding what was for him, no doubt, a stock-in-trade non sequitur:

"You know, I just got into directing to meet pretty girls."

"You can't fool me, sir," I said, remaining deferential. "I know it's not easy to pull off a shot like that. You must've loved the cinema."

"I never called it 'the cinema'!" Vic retorted, growing cranky again.

Our conversation continued to follow this strange pattern of give-and-take. I didn't succeed in getting him to take any credit for his work.

Vic's personal assistant and bodyguard was a man named Manolito, Manolito Gallo. He was a well-built man, greying at the temples, and wearing a large cross which rose to the level of bling. He laughed good-naturedly at Vic's pretty girl remark despite the fact he must have heard it a hundred times himself. Then it apparently drew near the time to feed Vic his meds or something, because I saw Manolito looking at his watch and becoming restless.

"He's my good-luck charm," Vic stated, catching me glancing at Manolito. "Been by my side since the beginning, right Manny?"

Manolito nodded and said, "Sure."

A long, awkward pause followed.

My thoughts wandered. I speculated that the religious fervor of his assistant may have had something to do with this old schlock-horror director's present reluctance to talk about his films. Or perhaps Vic was drawing close enough to the end of life to start catching a glimpse of that heavenly light himself.

Vic finally interrupted my train of thought.

"You should talk to Scott Sliden," he offered, somewhat apologetically. "He was my AD back then."

"Scott Sliden the agent?"

"That's the one."

3

Scott Sliden had always been deferential to reviewers. He had lobbied me personally a few times on behalf of clients, and I had run into him "accidentally" on more than one opening night. But I never crossed the line into that quid-pro-quo business of trading swank lunches or comp tickets for critical stars; I've maintained my standards.

The next time I saw Scott, I remembered Victor Tata and mentioned I'd seen him recently.

I swear, Scott's eyes watered a little.

"Vic was like a father to me when I was in kind of a bad place in my life. Tell you about it some other time."

He paused awkwardly, and then asked:

"How's the old guy doing?"

I didn't share with Scott the impression I had received from my visit of a sadly depleted man afraid that his time was just about up.

"He's getting by."

I repeated to Scott the gist of the conversation, however, asking if he had any clue why Vic would forward all questions about the opening scene of *Hell's Picnic* to him.

"It's funny, you know—I still wonder about that sequence myself sometimes," he replied. "All Vic would ever repeat was, 'It must have been the hand of God.'"

"He used that same phrase with me!"

"Yeah, well, you know, Vic was never the most religious guy. Known more for those visits to actresses in their trailers for late-night 'rehearsals.' Had a thing for redheads . . . ."

The scene, Scott, the scene.

"Well, I remember lining everybody up and finding them their places, but Vic's storyboard sketch was just that—very sketchy. You know, I don't even recall him calling for action."

He continued: "I was standing behind a kind of grassy knoll halfway down the hill, and Vic was supposed to signal me with his arm from the top, like a general. But I never got the signal, M.V."

"I swear I wasn't the one to call for action," he added. "Talk to H. J. Brown if you don't believe me."

"H. J. Brown the actor?"

"That's the one."

I had to wonder then just how many careers *Hellish Picnic* had launched!

"I represent him, you know. He's been lying low for a while. Let me punch his number into your phone for you?"

I handed my phone over to Scott Sliden. In for a penny, in for a pound, I suppose.

But by now, I was more curious than ever to solve the riddle of *Hellish Picnic*.

4

H. J. Brown was certainly not the most gifted talent in the industry—none of these guys ever were—but he had achieved a measure of success as an action-adventure character actor. He had played drug dealers, hit men, and once, to some minor acclaim, a high school bully-turned-football player who deliberately maims opposing players, in the aptly named "blockbuster" *Concussed* (1997).

I had never spoken with him. I couldn't have told you beforehand if he was the type of actor to lie through his teeth or to keep it real.

Fortunately, it was the latter.

"Great scene, man!" he blasted over the phone when I mentioned I would like to ask him a couple of questions about the opening of *Hellish Picnic*.

It took me a while to get him to focus.

"Scottie had me on a hair-trigger," H. J. elaborated. "He could get really carried away with the walkie-talkie."

"That day I was stationed at the bottom of the hill with the extras, you know, listening for him to whisper 'Now, now' in my ear so I could turn around and shout 'Rolling!' to start the scene.

"Scottie had this habit of saying 'Places . . . get ready . . .' and then playing with his Motorola, clicking the Talk button on and off. I would be hanging on for a super long time before I got the word.

"I guess, what do you expect, a first-time director and a first-time AD, they didn't have their timing down. Sometimes I thought I would hear Scottie say 'Now!' before he mashed the button, and have to catch myself."

"So, you're telling me, the scene started by accident?"

"Yeah, but it's weird. I remember being in deep shit a couple of times for yelling 'Rolling!' too early, but this time I swear it wasn't me!

"I wish I could take the credit, man! Whoever made that call really picked his moment well."

"So, who was it, then, if not you? Was there a second-second AD?"

"Nah. We were too low-budget in those days."

I waited.

"Here's the weirdest thing. The whole atmosphere at the park suddenly changed. A strange breeze came up or something. It got quiet. Then this deep voice echoed out from behind the pavilion.

"It sounded like, 'Rooolling!'

"Maybe it was the script we were shooting, but that voice didn't even sound like a live human. All at once, everyone just started moving. It was like we were under some mysterious control.

"I know it sounds weird. But that's the way it went down."

"So who do you think gave the command?"

"I never found out, man! I was curious but freaked out at the time. After we cut, I walked around back, but there was no one there but a couple of the grips. I asked Manny later what he'd seen, but he said nothing."

"Manny?"

"One of the grips, man."

I had a strange thought. "Was his name, by any chance, Manolito?"

"Yeah, yeah, some Mexican guy from Argentina. Hispanic I mean," H. J. added, a trifle embarrassed.

"I think I might know him."

"He's still hanging around, you know—now he's like Vic's personal assistant. Really into the God thing."

I had another minor inspiration at this point.

"H. J., a final question. Did you ever hear Vic use the expression 'the hand of God'?"

"Vic? You got to be kidding. That guy was one of the original playas from way back. But you know . . ."

"What?"

". . . I think I did hear Manny say it."

"Manny did?"

"It was regarding that day on the set, after the rest of us had gotten our asses chewed out by Vic. Boy howdy, I never saw Vic angrier than that.

"That is, at least until he saw the dailies and realized he had filmed this genius scene!"

5

So now it was down to Manny.

"Tell it to me straight, amigo. Were you perhaps the uncredited director of that opening scene? Did you yell out, *'Rolling*?"

"Me, *señor?*"

We sat by the edge of Vic's pool. Vic was inside taking his afternoon nap. The pool had probably been the site of some splendid out-of-control parties in the glory days, but it had now been a decade or more since Vic had, in any sense, danced with the devil. It badly needed a paint job and a couple of tiles were cracked and coming loose.

Poor Vic—any royalties from the *Hellish* series were almost certainly dwarfed by his Social Security check.

"Don't you remember?" I asked Manny.

"Sure, I remember the day of that shoot well: June 22, 1986."

I paused, somewhat taken aback. "OK, so how could you possibly know that?"

"England vs. Argentina—World Cup, Mexico.

"More than anything else, I wanted to catch this game, *señor*. It wasn't too long after the Falklands and we were looking for payback."

"So?"

"I was lying on the grass behind the pavilion with one of the guys watching the game on portable TV. I wasn't going to stop watching for anyone, not even for Mr. Vic!"

"Do you know this game?" he asked.

"I can never remember World Cup years," I said. "Wait a minute—I think I do. Wasn't that the game Diego Maradona scored two goals?"

"*Si*, Mr. M.V.! We like to think his second goal was the finest ever scored in match play, but his first goal was much more infamous."

Ah yes—now I remembered watching the footage, over and over, of Maradona's averted head and the subtly batted ball. It was a hand ball the referee had missed, and which the great Maradona himself later apologized for.

"And so, you're telling me . . ."

"When Maradona scored, I couldn't contain myself. I was so lost in this game and didn't know how close it was to filming.

"I turned the sound all the way up when the announcer shouted '*Goooal!*'"

"And . . . ?"

"And everyone thought we were rolling."

I smiled at Manny. *Lucky for Vic!*

Manny smiled back. He looked like a former athlete himself, easily able to lift the wasted old man in and out of his wheelchair. He was probably the only family Vic had left now. And he certainly no longer had anything to hide or any career to protect.

I had a hunch he did have one final thing to tell me, however.

Turns out, I was right.

"Do you know we have a nickname for that first goal Maradona scored, *señor?*"

"Oh?" I replied, not quite remembering.

"We like to call it, 'The Hand of God.'"

Well!

He added, as an afterthought: "As I understand it, my little mistake was perhaps not such a bad thing. Much good came of this scene for Mr. Vic's career."

"Perhaps," he speculated solemnly, fondling the cross around his neck, "one might even say that the Lord was at work, after all."

I was just rising to leave. Vic would be awake soon, awake to struggle through the remains of another day.

"But as for myself, *señor*, I don't believe God cares so much for wicked films about devils!"

THE ARTIST OF THE DEAD

1

I hardly recognized Hap Udall when I ran into him near the San Lorenzo marketplace in Florence. He was decked out in a beret and rimless sunglasses and sporting a goatee.

Hap was a former film student of mine, originally from Utah, who had gone on to author one of the better-selling books in the "for Imbeciles" series, *Screenwriting for Imbeciles*.

Despite our past connection, and the fact Hap's text conveniently incorporated several of my own screenwriting exercises, I had never ordered it for my undergraduate classes. Call me old fashioned (I am), but I can't quite condone anything for academic use that boldly proclaims mastery of an art form can be achieved by following a highly reductive set of steps, or by gazing at text boxes which simulate online pop-ups.

Still, even with that successful early publication under his belt, I don't believe Hap would have struck anyone in his graduating class as a budding aesthete. So his new appearance surprised me, as did his slightly brusque manner.

"*Buongiorno,* Dr. M.," he greeted me. "I don't have a lot of time to talk right now, but let's get together soon."

I said sure, I would be staying in town another week. Was he traveling?

"No, researching. I'm working on a project, something *big*."

"Another textbook?"

Hap didn't respond, only waving me off as though I had suggested something entirely beneath his dignity.

We exchanged numbers and agreed to meet the next day for breakfast at a little trattoria off the Via Alfani.

2

"I'm here to view the *Cancello Dei Traditori* of Alessio Coretti," Hap announced.

"Do you know it?"

"Ah yes, Coretti," I said. His 'Traitor's Gate.'"

"How *well* do you know it?"

I pulled up my mental picture. Not hard to do: the famous painting featured a memorable tableau of grotesque bodies, contorted by hideous tortures, nailed to a city gate. Above were other heads impaled on pikes, mouths and tongues protruding as though the victims had been garroted to death.

Several figures were distorted to the point that they looked almost inhuman. One dominated the center plane of the painting, its lower jaw horribly distended. Picture an image akin to Edward Munch's *The Scream,* only more realistically depicted; then consider, if you would care to, what cruel means it would actually take to contort a human visage so.

It was the kind of artwork hard to get out of your head, a grim and graphic reminder of man's inhumanity to man.

"One of Coretti's later works, I believe. Past his golden period, after he had grown weary of painting cherubim for the Pope."

"That's right, but do you know the source?"

I confessed I didn't. I had thought the painting a work of dark imagination and said as much.

"Yeah, well, it isn't. Such a gate once actually existed in the former principality of Fioreli, not too far from here. It was said that the sight of the gate was so terrible, even the Medici left the city alone!"

"That's interesting," I said. "So you're here to research the painting?"

"Not the painting, the gate," Hap said. "And Fra Baldesarre de Fioreli."

I confessed I'd never heard of him.

"He's only the greatest artist who ever lived!"

Hap was now looking at me with a slight air of condescension.

"He was the hero who saved the city from the Medici. He created the gate."

I squinted at a postcard version of Coretti's *Cancello Dei Traditori* Hap had brought along.

In truth, the bodies created such a distraction it was hard to make out many details of the structure itself. It looked pretty standard-issue 14th or 15th Century to me. But I tried to be polite.

"Built solid to keep intruders out, I see. Though one look at the way the prince treated his enemies would probably have done the trick, too!"

"Exactly, exactly," Hap replied, growing as enthused as his new sense of cool would allow. "But Fra Baldesarre didn't design the gate. He sculpted the bodies!"

"He sculpted them?"

"Yes! The title of the book I'm working on is *The Artist of the Dead*. It's about Fra Baldesarre, how this poor monk-sculptor with no political aspirations and little training was called on to help defend the city by creating a spectacle. It was the only recourse the prince had. His fighting forces were almost nil, his city about to be rolled over by the Medici.

"So, what he came up with is the next best thing—a really good scare.

"He commissioned Fra Baldesarre to fashion sculptures and assign them demonic or animal features, like gargoyles, along with bodies to suggest horrible deaths under torture. Keep in mind that in the Coretti, we're only dealing with a copy, and then you may get some feel for the original impact."

Needless to say, I was quite impressed by all of this, and praised Hap Udall unreservedly for his book concept.

"What a story to tell whenever one is challenged that the Gothic cannot be high art," I commented, "or that ghouls and goblins exist only to make young children behave."

"Exactly!" Hap said again, beaming. "Here was an artist who devoted himself to his community, who literally saved his city through art.

He was growing enthusiastic, starting to show traces of the genial old Hap.

Then he suddenly checked himself.

"Dr. M., just one thing. I have to swear you to secrecy on this. This book is going to be important! It's only by pulling some major strings I've been granted access to the Vatican Library to examine papers mentioning Fra Baldesarre."

"That's where I'm headed next," he added. "I've already viewed the painting and taken pictures of the site where the gate once stood."

"That must have been inspiring!" I exclaimed.

"It's now a goat pen," Hap replied in disgust.

3

It turns out that I didn't catch up with Hap Udall again for a couple of years. When I did, it was at a Barnes & Noble for a book signing.

A headshot of a smiling Hap immediately caught my attention. As the time elapsed since Italy seemed about right for a release of the Fra Baldesarre opus, my eyes raced over the announcement. Then I caught the title of Hap's new release, *Art History for Imbeciles,* and felt an immediate letdown.

When it comes to art, I really am a stickler. I think we should all make an effort to lift ourselves up to the Sister Wendy level, at least.

It didn't comfort me any to spot Hap surrounded by fans congratulating him anew for boiling down aesthetics to a few basic precepts.

Hap had sloughed off the beatnik look and wore an immaculate blue sport coat with designer chinos. He looked just about ready to put in a TV appearance, and perhaps he was, for he was signing books so fast it looked like exercise.

When I joined the end of the line and approached the table, his elbow was already cocked for the next signature.

True, I hadn't bought a book and have no right to complain; but if I had, I think I would have been a little miffed that Hap hadn't first asked about signing it for my Aunt Gladys or for anyone else.

He looked up suddenly, startled to see me standing there.

"I'll take the one about Fra Baldesarre, if you've got it," I offered.

Hap blushed. "I don't. But I would like to talk with you, if you've got a minute."

4

"Search turn up empty?" I asked, over coffee.

Jacket off, Hap was now looking a little more sullen and needed a prompt.

"Oh, no," he replied, rewinding his thoughts back to where he had left matters with me in Florence. "Turns out, there was a whole trove of letters and papers at the Vatican."

"Fra Baldesarre had been excommunicated," Hap added, "and that can be a long, drawn-out process."

"Excommunicated? For what reason?"

"You know, at first I thought it was for profanity. My Italian was not too good—I was using Google Translate.

"There was certainly a lot in there, at first, about art and sacred depictions, how the content of sculptures must serve a divine purpose."

"Didn't Baldessare explain to the Holy Fathers how he had helped save his city from destruction? Or was this another case of the Holy Roman Empire growing greedy to annex another territory, and perceiving that Baldesarre and the prince were standing in their way?"

"Maybe a little of that, too," Hap said, looking slightly troubled.

"It's been a while since I've read my Machiavelli," he apologized.

"Anyway, while digging through the boxes, I eventually found an early sketch of Coretti's painting. That's when I learned he had originally been sent to Fioreli by the Vatican on a kind of spy mission to record the appearance of the gate as carefully as possible. Which explains why the later painting could be rendered in such detail, in a manner highly unusual for its period."

"Interesting. So Coretti himself never left the Vatican fold."

"Nope, never," Hap replied.

"Would you like to see the sketch?" he asked. "I have a copy on file."

Hap punched up Coretti's drawing on his ever-handy tablet.

Superimposed over the original, yellowed image were Hap's white outlines of the bodies from the "Traitor's Gate" painting.

He had marked these with individual numbers, and at the bottom of the screen popped up a numbered list of names.

Hap's expression grew darker.

"Those, I'm very sorry to say, turn out to be actual citizens whose bodies Coretti discovered on the gate. I looked them up: they were all mentioned in the trial record as prominent officials of Fiorela."

He paused for a moment, staring down at the table.

"Over the years, the throng of visitors to the gate grew larger and larger. Sightseers arrived in horse-drawn carts or by foot, sometimes carrying picnic lunches and making a full day of it, but always demanding an ever-more gruesome spectacle.

"Fra Baldesarre had indeed begun his career as a sculptor. Somewhere along the line, however, as his art became a major attraction, he must have gotten carried away with his own celebrity. Or he simply ran out of ideas.

"Eventually, he began to replace some of the sculpted bodies with real ones, updating the gate every month or two."

"All of which," Hap added, "is bad enough."

Here he paused, somewhat dramatically, to let this little teaser sink in.

"Originally, the sculptor must have obtained new bodies from the morgue, dressed them down, and posed and arranged them on the gate.

"But when no suitable corpses were forthcoming, and others began to whisper his work had lost its impact, Fra Baldesarre suddenly decided to change course. Coldly and diabolically, he began to designate his own subjects, offering up the names of his critics or of alleged conspirators to the prince.

"Under the circumstances, or perhaps because he himself was afraid to question a popular and powerful public figure, the prince felt obliged to gratify Baldessare by supplying him with fresh artistic materials."

Hap noticed the scowl spreading on my face.

"Believe it or not, it gets much worse. During the trial, a direct suggestion was made to Fra Baldesarre that perhaps he hadn't just waited to receive bodies from the prince, as earlier claimed.

"Rather, out of a warped sense of artistic pride, that he had finally thrown off all reason and restraint and begun to actively take part in the tortures himself, even going so far as to direct the executioners in order to get just the expression he wanted on a finished corpse.

"He did not deny this charge, nor did he ever express any remorse for his victims before the Vatican fathers.

"In short, Fra Baledesarre was a proud, evil man, a treacherous murderer who betrayed his own countrymen!" Hap spat, with a crestfallen look on his face one only gets when disappointed by a former hero.

"So what happened to him?"

"Poetic justice, of a kind. He was tried, convicted, and tortured to death."

Hap paused again for a long time, then said, "Look again at the sketch."
I did.

"Now compare it with the later painting," he continued, pulling up that famous image in another window.

I again examined the sketch, this time alongside the painting, taking careful note of all the ovals with which Hap had marked positions of bodies.

A brief moment passed until I realized that one of the figures in Coretti's painting was nowhere to be found in the original sketch the artist made of the gate.

It was the centerpiece of the whole work, the horrible visage of the man with the elongated jaw and protruding tongue.

"In his painting, that good man of unwavering faith, Coretti, actually sought to offer to posterity a stern warning," Hap explained.

"He did so by choosing to give central position to the most infamous traitor of them all—the one who had betrayed his countrymen, his faith, and his art, and who later paid the ultimate price for wicked pride."

"You mean?" I asked.

"Yes. That hideous corpse is the treacherous Fra Baldesarre himself."

THE EVAN CHRONICLES

1

My friend Evan is acting in a film set in Sarajevo. In it, his character reaches a point of despair and becomes a petty thief, taking a flashlight and smashing through a jewelry store window in an industrial complex containing both a church and a McDonald's. His accomplice, a young towheaded hood, pressures him to do the job.

I thought Evan's character motives might have been slightly more idealistic, perhaps something to do with money-changing near a temple. But the two are detected and the police move in. We see them herded off awkwardly and Evan saying, "Ow!"

2

Ranging over the set of a *Gone with the Wind* remake, I briefly lend a hand to some grips who hold up a screen, then stoop to scrape some resin off the wood floor of an old auditorium. It is being converted into an antebellum dance hall.

Evan's wife, playing Scarlett, comes out and starts making demands about how she must be shot. She insists that her face be highlighted in different sparkling colors, and then retreats into her dressing room.

So I put out a call to the director of photography.

I continue to circle. Young debs step out one-by-one in ballroom dresses, and finally Evan's wife reappears in the arms of her dancing partner.

I am going to tell her the DP has been summoned, but am gently led aside by another crew member. He raises his finger to his lips and points to the two dancers.

They have passed through that looking glass and are now in character.

3

I'm not able to do much of anything right on the set. The screenwriter hands me an accordion folder containing some important memorabilia, and I misplace it. Then Evan asks me to watch his little daughter, who drops her doughnut on the carpet, picks it up, and starts to take a bite. I hold her arm for a second and examine the doughnut. It looks OK to me. But Evan comes over, frowning, and pulls a thin carpet fiber off the end of it. He shakes his head and returns to the shoot.

The little girl tells me she wants to act, just like her French mother. She sits in a folding chair and pretends she is an elderly *grand-mère*. She points to the craft service table and asks me to bring her more "*médication*."

Dutifully I fetch another doughnut and feed a piece of it to her, but it is the wrong kind, with nuts, and the girl starts to make a fuss. She spits the chunk on the floor and proceeds to make gagging noises.

This time Evan is over like a shot, yelling. His daughter glares at me and sticks out her tongue.

4

Mercifully—or perhaps not—Evan assigns me to work on a little writing project.

The topic concerns the career of two old film actors who had once starred in an original musical production. Each man tells me hopelessly glorified anecdotes to put in my book and attempts to control the discussion.

Obviously, they have very little confidence in my research abilities. But then I locate a passage in a previous source describing how the two had liked to toss a frisbee during breaks from shooting.

So when they ask me, somewhat paranoically, what I intend to write about next, I reply, a little defiantly, "On frisbee."

5

Evan throws me a little birthday party in my apartment. Typical gesture, generous but with a catch: no clean-up for him.

Never a too-hearty partier, I take a nap.

When I awake, the wind is howling outside. A few party guests still mill around although Evan is long gone. So I fall into the host's role.

I notice one mysterious young woman—very dark hair, attractive. She is intrigued by a reference book I have on witches.

She opens the volume to an entry about "Wicked Lucy" and tells me she wants to borrow it because her name is also Lucy.

I ask her where she is from. She says, "I'm your Anima."

6

Evan is visiting my screenwriting class but says he isn't feeling well and must depart, disappointing several students prepared to bombard him with questions.

Not long afterwards, his old college girlfriend shows up, then a more recent mistress, then an old family friend, then a person claiming to be his stepbrother John, though I have met Evan's family many times and never heard anyone speak of him.

Later, I get a phone call from Evan himself, nervous.

I tell him about the retinue of visitors to my class and the man masquerading as his brother. He doesn't reply.

Suddenly, I sense Evan might not have disclosed his full history to me after all. I tell him if there is a rift, it seems John wants to heal it. No sense living with an old pain.

Evan finally responds, telling me the falling-out is more recent. I tell him I understand—these things have a way of unraveling quickly.

But now I am the one who must get off the phone. I know nothing of the situation and have just about expended my whole stock of clichés.

7

Evan and I are driving around town with a location manager, scouting for an appropriate suburban house to use as a setting for a movie based on my book *Dream Koans.*

After hours of winding streets that circled back on each other, most with nicely kempt yards and homes, we finally find what we want: a house set back from the street with a wide porch and crawl space. A large oak looms over the yard, permitting only mottled sunlight, and one limb hangs threateningly over the roof. The lawn is dotted with dandelions and crabgrass.

We ring the bell.

It is answered by a middle-aged couple who do not appear too eager to talk—either with us or with each other.

The LM explains our purpose, the likely film dates, and the small remuneration involved. At that, the man's interest seems to increase slightly.

His wife, on the other hand, is not looking too pleased. "For what kind of movie is this?" she asks.

Evan nods toward me. "It's a drama," I say, "a little creepy-scary, about strange doings afoot in suburbia . . . ."

"I knew it!" the woman interjects, giving her husband a withering look. "I told him to get his sorry ass out there and cut the grass!"

8

Evan is asleep, so I believe this will be a good time to sneak out and get us some coffee.

He and I are finally going to get it done—adapt one of his many screenplay concepts into a useable treatment he can shop around. It has taken us a few years to get together because we now live on opposite coasts. We stay at a timeshare cottage he rarely uses and have reunited at the airport just the night before.

When I go to check the refrigerator, it is empty, of course. But I recall seeing an old bike leaning up against the side of the place and figure I might as well get some exercise and solve our caffeine deficit disorder at the same time.

The sun is just coming up when I return, laden with a thermos.

Evan is standing next to his rental car, speaking on the phone to his agent. He takes the thermos from me without a word and nods. Then he tells the caller no problem, he can be back in LA in a few hours.

9

Evan has finally completed a book of memoirs with a ghostwriter. It has been dedicated "To My Pals," and I am being interviewed on cable TV.

"You were one of the 'Two Michaels' mentioned in the book as being important influences—" my questioner begins.

Hardly a question yet—nor a very promising lead-in to one.

"—do you think the Dedication is to you?"

I politely pretend to consider this inane speculation carefully, but actually I am just trying to think of a topper.

"No," I finally reply. "The book is dedicated to pals everywhere, to all those who are willing to stop and be a pal to someone in need."

10

I am making a connection through LAX with my stepson Yonas. Out of the blue, I decide to call Evan.

There are noises in the background and I can't tell for a moment whether someone has picked up the phone. Then Evan's voice comes in loud and clear.

"We'll have to have you over to the house—you see, we're having a party," he says.

He sends a limo to pick us up.

By the time we arrive, the house is full of guests. One man there I know, an old college friend of mine and Evan's. He is upbeat because he thinks Evan might get him a job in which he can "use his photography." He shows me a portfolio of his recent work—shots of bones done for a scientific publication. The bones are faintly outlined in indigo.

The houseguests gather around the home theater console, and all of the seats fill quickly.

A new movie begins to play featuring an absent-minded superhero. Evan is a co-producer.

After we watch for a while, Evan's new wife notices Yonas beginning to nod off and offers to give up her chair, but I tell her we are fine.

I briefly consider asking her about an overnight stay but know it will be far less complicated simply to head back to the airport early.

And so, before any of the other guests can make off with the limo, I pick up the small sleeping boy, nod to my hosts, and step outside.

THE DOUBLE DARE DEVIL

1

It was quite an impressive scene. On a concrete parapet forty stories overhead, the Vice President of the United States scrambled to escape from two terrorists.

Fortunately, from the left of frame, the action hero Douglass McCracken entered. He grabbed the veep by the tie with one hand and threw some good old-fashioned jabs at the masked goons with the other. He didn't seem at all conflicted about launching them into space with a roundhouse punch and a well-placed judo kick. I watched the two figures float down the side of the building, legs and arms dangling. A crane-mounted camera tilted down to follow their progress, and then I heard "Cut!" yelled just before they crash-landed onto a giant, pink foam cushion.

It looked like a soft landing, but you can never tell.

With apologies to McCracken fans, on that day it was possibly the edifice itself which had done the best job of acting.

For the movie *McCracken V: Let Freedom Reign*, directed by Rocco Testi, a nondescript Phoenix bank building had been remodeled in the likeness of the new Freedom Tower in New York, scheduled to open the following year.

Even on a reduced 1:5 scale, the elongated triangles of the cable-net glass façades were impressive, jutting into the sky like shining obelisks.

It made you wonder if skyscrapers were designed just with Hollywood blockbusters in mind.

2

If you like Westerns or old action movies, you may have seen Skip Eubanks in a dozen or so films without being aware of it.

He's stunt-doubled for some of the biggest action stars in the industry but is usually long gone from a movie before it wraps. And no matter what death-defying feat he and his company perform, you can bet someone handling PR for the film—or for a star whose image might need a little rehabilitating or toughening-up—will leak some nonsense to the press about the stunts "being real," performed by the lead himself. Don't believe a word of it. It was probably Skip, or someone like Skip.

Skip Eubanks started out in Arizona as a poor man's Evel Knievel, billing himself as the "Double Dare Devil" and traveling the Southwest state fair and carnival circuit.

He had smashed up motorcycles, cars, trucks; been shot out of a cannon and engulfed in rings of flame; and, not too surprisingly, spent much of his twenties in a body cast before making the successful transition to Hollywood.

I had never met Skip personally, but during my short flight to Phoenix to report on the McCracken flick, read some PR about the "most death-defying stunts ever attempted" and thought I would make some enquiries.

Ordinarily, this would have been difficult because the Italian action film director Rocco Testi was notoriously close-lipped when it came to the media. It was no doubt a defensive posture—his work was generally panned by critics. However, it happens that I did know his second cameraman, my nephew Garrett Ho, who usually worked fairly closely with the stunt people.

Garrett's own dream, naturally, was to direct. And I could, with some little effort, foresee a future for him in that field, notwithstanding my own nepotism and tendency to uncritically praise his thoughtful attention to detail and talent for cinematography.

But I also knew it would be very difficult for Garrett to make the leap from behind the camera to the director's chair. In a word, he was a little too unassuming—and too nice.

"Hey Uncle Mike," he answered when I rang him up.

As I dodged around the terminal to preserve the weak phone signal, I told Garrett I was interested in visiting him on the set.

"Sure, it's a good time for it," he responded. "We're shooting outside all week."

Garrett invited me to stay with him at the crew's hotel, but I demurred. He then suggested I join him in the lobby that night—but by then, he was yawning.

I could tell he had been working eighteen-hour days every day for weeks on end and needed his sleep. So I told him to go to bed.

"Well, bring your safety goggles tomorrow," Garrett said. "We're going to be blowing up a ton of stuff!"

"Any chance I can meet Skip Eubanks while I'm there?"

"Skip? I think you mean his wife, Bonnie."

"Why her?"

"Skip's not doing much talking these days."

3

It turns out I was doubly in luck that first afternoon. With the street still blocked off, the crew prepared to shoot a second scene. In it, McCracken teams up with his young sidekick to blast more terrorists, this time with a flamethrower mounted on a Humvee.

This scene, which would account for perhaps seven or eight seconds of actual running time, took more than three hours to set up. It had to be filmed in one take because four terrorists were going to be set ablaze. Both first and second camera crews were present so nothing would be missed.

Curious, I watched as four stunt men wearing black Ninja outfits emerged from the EUBANKS AND SONS team bus where they had been prepped and took their places in front of the ersatz Freedom Tower set.

Just out of frame, two fire trucks and hundreds of crew members and curious onlookers waited. I found a place behind a traffic barrier guarded by a young production assistant.

Finally, there came the moment when Rocco Testi's first AD screamed for quiet. A flurry of activity spread through the crew. A few beats later, the diminutive director himself stepped forward and yelled, *"Azione!"*

Panicked shouts rose in the street, and a carefully positioned throng of extras parted like the Red Sea for the speeding Humvee.

From his position atop the back, McCracken snarled as he spotted the terrorists trying to escape and shouted down to his sidekick to drive closer.

"Burn in hell!" he yelled, emptying the contents of the flamethrower.

The terrorists, their costumes no doubt previously prepped with flammable liquid, burst immediately into fireballs.

McCracken raised a fist in the air.

Testi yelled "Cut!" and the onlookers applauded.

Pleased, the little director seemed to acknowledge their presence for the first time, tipping his hat.

Meanwhile on the set, there was controlled pandemonium.

A rescue crew arrived with fire hoses, dousing the fireballs until they contracted down to human size.

Three of the stunt men were writhing in pain on the ground while the fourth lay unmoving and unconscious.

There were audible gasps.

EMTs from Skip Eubanks' crew quickly circled the man and carried him off toward the bus.

I wondered briefly whether I would have another kind of piece to write that night for my editor, one titled "Tragedy on the Set," when for the first time I noticed a large woman barking orders to the Eubanks team.

She stepped forward and hardly glanced at the fallen man before telling the others to stop dallying and carry him away.

Garrett approached her, his face a tragic mask of concern, but she cut him off immediately with a curt, "He's fine. He's a professional."

She turned around abruptly and tromped back to the bus.

4

That would be Bonnie Eubanks, Skip's wife.

The following morning, Garrett arranged for me to meet with her and Skip in their little trailer.

The trailer was parked on a somewhat seedy motel lot next to the team bus. The motel, located about twenty miles south of town, was where the two preferred to stay in lieu of more expensive accommodations. Beyond it were a gas station and a hot wings place.

Bonnie was a woman with long, ash-blond hair in her mid-fifties wearing jeans that fit her a little too tight, and a EUBANKS AND SONS tank top that revealed some biker tattoos.

I saw a flaming motorcycle, a few skulls, and the bright coils of a cobra encircling her neck. The mouth of the snake opened just under her chin, the fangs appearing to slice into her jugular and trailing little droplets of blood-red ink toward her clavicle.

Bonnie offered me some strong coffee and assured me that Enrico was fine now, just resting. He would be ready for more action soon.

Enrico?—Ah. From the number of stuntmen on the team (about twenty), I should already have guessed that "Eubanks and Sons" was just a name.

I told Bonnie I was relieved, and expressed the hope I might interview the man himself later.

"He doesn't speak any English," Bonnie snapped, trying to dismiss my suggestion. "And I don't let my guys talk to reporters. Trade secrets."

I changed the subject, inquiring instead about Skip.

Although the former stuntman was in the room with us, he wasn't able to speak and his eyes appeared glazed and unfocused. Sadly, he had seen his last workday several years prior when he was paralyzed from the waist down in a fall from a helicopter.

Bonnie had taken over the operation then.

"He has his good days and his bad days," she observed.

Then she must have caught me looking at Skip's left arm, which seemed incongruously large compared to the rest of his withered body.

"In his glory days as the Double Dare Devil, Skip broke every bone in his body, you know—all except for that one arm.

"He was always proud of it, wasn't you, Three-D?" she continued, with something approaching real affection.

Skip didn't react to the mention of his nickname.

"It must be hard for you to carry on without him," I sympathized. "Training in all those new recruits yourself must take a lot of work."

"Skip always said, 'It don't take no genius to be a stunt double,'" she retorted. "That to go the extra mile, sometimes you just gotta park your brain at the door."

What happened next was an interruption which might well have been preplanned.

Rico, Bonnie's bilingual assistant, came in murmuring something about the guys being hungry.

I wanted to inquire again about visiting with the stuntman who had suffered a near-tragedy, but Bonnie stood up and I knew the interview was over.

Still, I thought I would ask.

"Any way I could have a quick word with Enrico before you pull out?"

"Not a chance, mister."

5

As I pulled out of the motel parking lot, I observed a little scurrying around the EUBANKS AND SONS bus and what looked like a "family" squabble erupting among Bonnie and Skip's many stage sons.

A couple of young men were arguing volubly with Rico. No longer costumed, the men were dressed in shabby work clothes. I got the impression that it might not have been long since either of them had crossed the border.

The border crossing was perhaps no more than a hundred and fifty miles away from where the bus was now parked. I looked to the south, seeing nothing there but an empty farm field.

Driving back to Phoenix, I communicated a few of my impressions to Garrett.

"I don't think these guys are very professional, after all," I told him. "If you ask me, they seem more like cannon fodder. But it's hard to gain access to them with Bonnie and Rico hovering around the bus all the time."

"I was there when the company was hired," Garrett informed me, "when Bonnie insisted Eubanks and Sons always worked exclusively with its own team of trainers and EMTs. The producers really read her the riot act and had her sign off on the liability."

"Good thing. I don't think Bonnie worries too much about insurance herself, not so long as she can find a steady supply of cheap labor."

"It sounds like exploitation!" Garrett replied, finally rousing himself and discovering some inner ire. "Someone should blow the cover on their operation."

"Well, you've been waiting for your own chance to direct, haven't you?"

"Aw, Uncle Mike, I just couldn't," he replied, conflicted. A moment passed in which Garrett seemed to be revisiting a private argument with himself.

"What's the latest word on Enrico?" he finally asked.

"I have a very, very bad feeling about Enrico."

6

Another day, another brutal scene. *Let Freedom Reign* was going to culminate in a thoroughly blood-red, white, and blue sequence.

With my crowd of fellow-spectators, I watched as McCracken swung around an old bulldozer and lowered the shovel for a final wounded charge at a terrorist camp.

The hero dodged sniper bullets, broke through fortifications, and plowed into a small building where the evildoers were plotting their next attack, taking out a couple of unfortunate guards and triggering a whole chain of explosions.

My stomach churned as I once again witnessed the Eubanks crew spring into action. To me, the men who came out to drag off the bodies of the stuntmen now appeared more like body snatchers than EMTs. They blinked as though unused to the daylight and peered around the set shyly, as if a little camera-conscious.

Perhaps Bonnie has also recruited a few aspiring actors, I reflected.

This time, however, I noticed Garrett Ho swing the second camera around to follow the Eubanks crew off set.

When it comes to bearing witness, the camera only sees what it sees—which is more than I can say for you or for me.

7

EXT. FARM FIELD ADJOINING ARIZONA
MOTEL – EVENING.

Outside: Moonlit. Spooky.

From the parking lot of the motel, TWO MEN emerge carrying shovels
and a stiff bundle tightly wrapped in a woven blanket.

Slowly, they pick their way across the furrows until they reach a freshly
dug pit.

They lower the bundle. It now appears to be a BODY, hastily draped
for burial. In the near background are two or three mounds of recently-
turned earth that might also be graves.

Unceremoniously and wordlessly, the two men cover the body with dirt.

We see them look a little frightened, although perhaps not so much
by the eeriness of the night, or the ghoulish activity in which they are
engaged.

Instead, they glance furtively back in the direction of the motel, as if
scared by something or someone else they expect to find there.

Suddenly, a WOMAN'S SHRILL VOICE is heard off screen.

WOMAN'S VOICE (OS)

Git back in here!

8

The next morning at the motel, there was no sense in beating around the bush with Bonnie. She was already overseeing preparations for departure.

"You like turning migrant workers into corpses?" I asked her, point blank.

"Illegals," she said.

"Does that make a difference?" I shot back, not really wanting to debate politics.

She shrugged.

Bonnie Eubanks seemed surprisingly nonchalant for a cold-blooded killer. But I suppose, from her perspective, I was a nobody, with no significant connection to the *Let Freedom Reign* production. She had already collected her last paycheck, and I had only gained access at all today by lying about researching some of Skip's glory days and discovering some old memorabilia.

From his wheelchair, Skip made a little gasping noise.

Bonnie was prepping him for travel, wrapping a blanket around his neck to keep him warm.

"No more killing," I said. "No more bodies."

Bonnie spat and pulled a shotgun out from under the wheelchair.

"Oh, no?" she replied. "I think I see a dead man right here."

But in a flash, before she could pull the trigger, Skip's one good left arm shot out reflexively.

The gun barrel jerked upwards and discharged.

A hole appeared in Bonnie's neck right where the snake tattoo had been.

She collapsed, dead, to the floor.

9

There was a moment of silence. Then I yelled out angrily to Garrett: "I can't believe you let her get that far!"

"I got it all!" Garrett replied, excited.

Almost as an afterthought, he added, "Oh my gosh, you're OK, aren't you?"

He poked his head into the trailer.

I just glared.

Skip, who had somehow managed to summon enough strength for a last stunt, now seemed to lose focus on the world again.

"Wait here just a minute, Uncle Mike. I need to get the police arrival," Garrett said, excusing himself.

I still wanted to kick his butt, but as he began to set up his tripod outside, I also couldn't help feeling a little proud of my nephew.

Garrett was following his own script now, a script he was excitedly formulating in his head.

10

Garrett's script, if you don't already know, would eventually be titled *American Dreamers*. The film he made went on to win many critics' awards for Best Documentary.

Although *American Dreamers* started out with a recap of Skip's storied career and an exposé of Bonnie's operation, it went far beyond this, allowing some of the migrant workers who had been recruited by Rico to tell their own stories—how they had been lured by promises of becoming professional stuntmen or actors in the kind of action-adventure movies they had loved as kids.

There are scenes of direct address to the camera as the would-be stars share their painful histories. A few later traveled with Garrett on the festival circuit and spoke to appreciative film audiences there. So in a way, you could say their dreams did come true.

The police eventually pulled two more bodies from graves dug near the motel parking lot.

Between acceptance speeches, Garrett Ho made a fledging attempt to finance a follow-up documentary that would have attempted to reconstruct a list of all the blockbuster films Eubanks and Sons had worked on, to match the casualties depicted in their action sequences with local media archives and coroners' reports. Rico, of course, wasn't talking.

But the studios soon caught wind of the project and bought the rights. The last thing they needed was for their popular sellers to be reappraised, perhaps even vilified as snuff films and removed from stores and lucrative online archives.

And so, for the foreseeable future, it will be up to the fans of the action flicks themselves to decide whether the violent sequences they recall so fondly were strictly necessary and to contemplate possible human costs.

These days, Garrett is doing just fine. When the family gets together at Christmas, you can always count on him to tease me about my lone acting performance—or upon me, for that matter, to good-naturedly protest that I *wasn't* acting.

He now directs a TV show about a group of three Princeton friends who drift rather aimlessly through life after college. One is an investment broker, one an assistant professor, and one a clown who works birthday parties and visits children's hospitals. They all live together in the investment broker's house and have many zany times with their hot Guatemalan housekeeper and a pet pig named Algernon.

That Garrett. I love him, but he's such a little sellout!

II

ZOMBIE TRIPTYCH

1. the cornydog zombie

It was a *most* disgusting spectacle to behold. Seated across the trough with the other State Fair contestants was my cousin Winston, bib under chin, about to bite into his eleventh cornydog! A winner—or so it would appear.

The other contestants had mostly dropped out of the running, and I mean that literally: peaked skin, glazed eyes, pupils dilating to ping-pong ball size before hitting the deck. With just one notable exception.

This man looked like he was having a heart attack. And as it turns out, he was. We later found out he had actually expired before our very eyes on cornydog number nine. In retrospect, this makes his sudden resurgence a minute later even more surprising.

With a jerk, the man sat up, quite undead, and began growling in guttural fashion. I, ever on the alert for zombie outbreaks, was quickly put on the alert.

But the creature's initial reaction threw me. It returned to its place at the table and reflexively began to dig into the trough again; albeit with a confused, slightly cross-eyed expression on its face.

Winston glanced over at his competition without any fear. He had been in this spot many times before, as our defending state champion for three years running. With quick grace, he slid down cornydogs twelve and thirteen.

His newborn zombie foe seemed slightly perplexed by the outside breading before sensing the presence of barely-cooked meat of dubious origin inside and chomping all the way down to the wooden stick with supernatural force, shattering it.

Cornydogs ten, eleven, and twelve quickly met their fate. Then our zombie contestant, evidently sensing fresher prey, backed away from the table and headed straight toward Winston!

No doubt, my cousin's pudgy forearms must have proved an attractive sight to a carnivore-run-amok.

With another growl, the zombie grabbed Winston's wrist and twisted it hard, bringing the tackily tattooed skin up to its dripping lips.

Fortunately, the twelfth cornydog had done the thing in.

The zombie's already-glazed eyes glazed over still more, and it slumped to the ground, defeated.

Winston had won again!

2. evil jeeveses!

At a formal dinner. Many costumed monsters there, none of them real. By contrast, two British servants wearing natty uniforms definitely looked like they were resisting the urge to turn.

A young woman and I were left alone with them in the den at one point. Finally throwing off the chains of propriety, the servants made their move, growling like the sick parasites they truly were and then closing the door behind us and attacking.

I managed to escape, *mostly* unscathed. The young woman wasn't so lucky. I tried to pull her away from the scene but was blocked by one of the evil Jeeveses.

I was struck over the head and just barely managed to stagger out the door before blacking out.

Later, I awoke. I had been placed comfortably to rest on a chesterfield. The other guests were still milling about, and a banquet table had been loaded with fine dishes and hors d'oeuvres.

The two British servants came out, still dressed in their coattails and mumbling softly to one another. They looked just a shade undead, and quite guiltily satisfied. Stiffly, they resumed their assigned duties.

As for myself, I couldn't resist the urge to pick a large turkey leg off the table and wave it right in the senior one's face.

I said to him, accusingly, "You guys get enough to eat?!"

3. carnatine knowledge

Thin may always be in, but if you were to ask me, the young brunette cashier at the co-op looked *preternaturally* slender.

Her flesh was pale, paler even than mine. Her cheeks were gaunt, and she pursed her thin lips with disapproval as she rang up my order—package after package of farm-fresh calves' brains.

It was like she didn't even want to touch them to avoid absorbing any juice through her fingers.

"Something the matter?" I asked.

"So, are you on some kind of Paleolithic diet or something?"

"Not exactly," I said. "I take it you're not fond of meat?"

"It's . . . disgusting," she said, unable to check herself. "I'm a vegan."

"Disgusting, eh? A vegan, eh?" I muttered, glancing around.

Per usual, I had picked the right time of day to come into the store. The place was completely deserted. So I thought I would do both of us a favor.

I leaned over the counter and, grabbing the girl's arm, took a modest-size bite out of her bony shoulder.

"Sweetheart, you should never sass a zombie," I scolded.

She shrieked, of course, and next her face went through a whole kaleidoscope of contortions as she began to jerkily adjust to her new physiology.

I waited, perusing one of the free magazines by the counter. These things usually take a few minutes.

Suddenly, the girl's face relaxed into a stupid grin as she looked at me, then at the packaged meat in front of her, then at me again, then back down.

This almost never happens—it's not at all symptomatic—but I swear some color actually rushed *into* the young woman's face.

Mercifully, I opened one of the packages for her and placed her hand on the quivering skull-jelly of some unfortunate cow.

Immediately, she tore off a chunk and brought it to her lips—then another. Finally she was really off to the races, in a good old feeding frenzy.

"Yes," I said, stroking her hair back to keep it from getting mussed. "Eat. Brains. Brains are *goood!*"

TRACTATUS VICTUS-MORTUUS
Treatise on the Living Dead

Zombie Idealism

The relationship of a zombie to its former identity is, indeed, only an iconic one: but so caught up are we in the semblance of the former person, we often fail to perceive the creature for the shadow-being it is. Some might argue the dehumanized appearance of the mummy, wrapped in linens to the point of anonymity, is precisely what generates its terror; but the staying power of zombies and similar creatures suggests, contrariwise, what we ultimately find most monstrous is an image of ourselves.

Zombie Theodicy

If the hunger of a zombie possesses the qualities of being *insatiable, invariable,* and *irresistible,* clearly the creature cannot be construed as a volitional being, nor "evil" per se, for evil implies intent. Only in a weak sense might a zombie be considered an instrument of malice—yet, it is uncertain by what hand it is steered, or for what purpose; or whether the condition simply runs a natural course, like an earthquake or a plague. Hence it is specious to refer to a zombie as *evil.*

Zombie Paradox

If a zombie delivers a lethal bite to a human, and subsequently renders the victim undead (viz., by spreading the virus), does the zombie truly feast on a *person*? Further, how would the zombie know when, so to speak, the tipping point has been reached?

Zombie Economics

When zombies devour brains, leaving behind scant remains of a carcass which cannot then reanimate, the supply of potential victims is thereby diminished. Even if the feast is left unfinished—and, by happenstance, still another undead being is generated and set into motion—by definition, that new carnivore will likewise be a consumer. We must bear in mind that the supply of fresh meat can nowise be considered endless; on the contrary, it will likely have been reduced *a priori* by an inevitable parental reluctance to bring children forth into a dystopian future.

Zombie Equality

When referring to a zombie, we use the pronoun "it" interchangeably for an entity spawned from a corpse either male or female. Whereas we might speak of a "male body" or a "woman's body," it sounds incorrect to our ears to refer to a "male zombie" or a "man's zombie." Thus it seems fallacious to conclude, as so many cultures have for millennia, that it is the condition of being dead which finally renders all beings equal; rather, it is the condition of becoming undead.

Zombie Ontology

If brains comprise the essence of the thinking person and are gorged upon and swallowed whole, does there ever come a moment, before the tissue dies, when it might fairly be stated that the empty husk of the zombie *contains* or *embodies* the identity of the victim?

Zombie Epistemology

If a blow to a zombie's cranial cavity renders it useless, then surely the control center of said entity is in the head, and to the extent it may be thought capable of purposive action, it must be in the ability to recognize and track its prey; i.e., to "think" like a zombie.

Zombie Relativity

If a zombie is shot into space orbit, the velocity of the spacecraft relative to the speed of light would appear to be, for all experimental purposes, inconsequential. For the zombie cannot age, nor be fazed by a return to a much-changed world.

Zombie Nirvana

The eyes: dead. Inner self: extinguished. The cycle of reincarnation: shattered. Spiritual success of a kind, to be certain, but what is less clear is whether there could be any collective profit for zombies in world domination.

WITCH-HUNTER PUZZLES

Exercises in Unerring Logic

1) A man's corpse lies face down on the ocean shore. The face has turned blue, but there isn't sufficient water in the lungs to indicate drowning. On the knees are bruises and splinters. In a parking lot above the beach, an abandoned automobile is also discovered, hastily double-parked. The question is, how had the man met his end?

ANSWER: Make no mistake, some vengeful witch must have cast a spell upon this poor man to make him believe he was a fish! In this case, the power of suggestion was such that he believed he must return to water immediately, else expire. Dropping everything, he had driven straight to the nearest public beach. There he had abandoned his vehicle and stumbled out along the boardwalk, tripping once in utter exhaustion. With a final effort, the man crawled out toward the waves to quaff a desperate, life-giving draught—only to discover, much too late, that he was technically a freshwater fish.

2) A woman's body is found near a baby stroller in the park. There is no sign of a child. There are also no exterior traces of violence to the body, although a later autopsy report reveals a surprise: the woman's stomach contains a small mouse! What was the cause of death?

ANSWER: Grief, sadly. Unfortunately, on her walk through the park, this woman must have made an angry witch jealous. The witch then placed a double-hex on mother and child, making the woman believe she was an owl and transforming infant into rodent. Unable to resist her own predatory nature, the woman reflexively gobbled the mouse—only to realize, after the spell faded, how she had been duped by the old hag's treachery.

3) A man lies at the bottom of a scenic overpass, dead of a fall. It is a known fact he had last stopped at a highway rest area to snack on a bunch of delicious, ripe bananas.

ANSWER: More than likely, this man had been swatting at a cloud of fruit flies, which would have been attracted by the discarded peels. Unfortunately, one fly must have been a witch traveling in disguise who didn't care for the assault. She had cast a revenge spell, causing the man to believe that he, too, was a part of the swarm. And so when the others flew off, he haplessly followed.

THREE STORIES THAT END WITH EXCLAMATIONS

1. a mindful demise?

I gritted my teeth. The Atlanta traffic was, as usual, uncompromising. And today I had a special reason for arriving home promptly: the appearance at my home of Thich Nhat Hanh of the Unified Buddhist Church. It's not every day one breaks bread with a Nobel Laureate.

"Yes, he's here," said my aunt Winnie, "waiting just as patient as you please."

"Tell him I'm on my way and very much looking forward to our Zen conversation," I said.

"Okay. Shall I offer him anything to eat? He's so skinny!"

"You can certainly try."

A half hour later I called back to report on my progress.

"It won't be long now," I said. "How's the Most Venerable Mr. Hanh?"

"Well, he bowed and accepted a piece of bread, and he's been nibbling on the same crust for ten minutes now. I've never seen anything like it."

I chuckled as I explained to my aunt the practice of mindful eating, how Mr. Hanh believed "each morsel of bread is an ambassador from the cosmos."

"Humph," Aunt Winnie said. But I could tell she was interested.

I had grossly underestimated my travel time. When I next called back, I discovered my aunt had continued with her feeding regimen.

"Now he's sampling some green bean casserole," she informed me.

"Oh," I said, and then a split second later, almost missed my exit.

For a new thought had suddenly occurred: Aunt Winnie's green bean casserole was, at best, an acquired taste, certainly not for the faint of heart. If Mr. Hanh tried to be mindful of every bite . . .

His peaceful words came back to haunt me as I raced my car up the drive. How important it was to "recognize" each item of food, really concentrate . . . how one must tune out the rest of the world and focus all one's attention on each chew.

"Good God!" I exclaimed, bursting in through the front door. "Get that plate away from him!"

2. super bored

At the church sale, where I had offered to help tag some items, I was bored. So bored, in fact, I found it quite difficult to refrain from using my superpowers to escape.

Briefly I pretended to be interested in some old curios on a table near the far corner of the parking lot and felt my legs twitching to transport me away from the venue at super-speed. But a busload of Boy Scouts was unloading boxes nearby, and one of them might just be alert enough to spot me.

I tried to lose the crowd again by examining some old refrigerator boxes near the geranium garden. These contained junk, mostly, and old shoes and clothes.

If I could just hop into one when no one's looking, I thought, *I could use my super-tunneling abilities to flee.* Then thought better of it, because I would be the first one the church ladies would call to handle the giant mole problem and have to listen to them all over again. I'm an exterminator by trade.

Anyway, too late: Here were Mrs. Hale and Mrs. Hodges coming over to visit. I fidgeted, feeling as trapped as I might have if one of my super-foes had encased me in a cement and carbon steel casket.

"Didn't it turn out to be a lovely day for the sale?" Mrs. Hale offered.

"Yes, just glorious," Mrs. Hodges seconded her, before I could answer.

I could feel myself levitating just a little. Fortunately, the ladies weren't paying much direct attention to me.

"I think those linens would be just the thing to spruce up someone's home."

"Yes, a bachelor's."

"And that lamp just needs a man's touch."

"Yes, a handyman's."

Could I hold out much longer? Could you, reader? The high-tensile muscles of my thighs felt like two rockets preparing for blast-off.

"I declare, Mrs. Hodges, isn't that Miss Alcott over yon?"

"Yes, she's so sweet. And never married."

Reader, I was gone. I whooshed upwards, saying a silent prayer that my blur would be too quick for the old ladies to track through their bifocals. Later, I could always find time to make some excuse.

After circling the church skies twice, I got out of sight behind the steeple.

There, I tuned in my super-hearing for a moment to confirm that my secret identity had been safeguarded.

"Now where did that nice man, Mr. Miller, go?"

"We were just talking to him."

"I hope we didn't offend him."

"Shush, Marla, he might could hear you."

"Such an eligible young man. But always vanishing on a person."

"Yes, one minute here and the next minute . . ."

". . . Gone!!" both ladies giggled together.

3. the follow-up visit

As I sat in the chair at my chiropractor's office, I began to sweat. Gemma, the receptionist, had brought out a bill including many previously-undisclosed charges. Apart from the fifteen-dollar copay for the appointment itself, there was a fee for plastic gloves, a strip of tape, a thermometer sleeve, and "Other/Miscellaneous" items totaling twenty-six dollars.

When Gemma returned to the lobby, I started to ask questions. She looked suddenly stricken with guilt for the charges, which she acknowledged she should have informed me of first. She darted back to the reception area, where I saw her bend low as if retrieving something furtively from a drawer or purse.

Rather shakily, she returned to me and began to count out twenty-six dollars, mostly in ones. For a brief moment, I felt guilty myself.

"I really appreciate it," I said to her.

At this, Gemma smiled and perked up. Then she placed a customer comment card in my palm. At the top I saw written the words: **"*How're We Doin???*"** Below that, a couple of dozen boxes to check.

"I hope you will give our office lots of '*Great*'s," she said.

"Sure," I replied. "I'll just take that survey with me."

"Oh," Gemma said, looking slightly disappointed again.

Upon returning home, I emptied my pockets and never even looked at the card.

That afternoon, I was lounging on the couch when I heard a big engine roar and a bright horn honk in the drive. Reluctantly, I got up and went to the door.

"Congratulations!" boomed a voice.

My eyes adjusted to the brighter light of outdoors. When they focused, I recognized a familiar face. It was Doctor Sven.

The chiropractor was a short, graying man with a goatee and perfect bronze tan. He grinned as he held out a huge bouquet of balloons, candy suckers, and plastic streamers. The streamers were so long that to prevent them from dragging, he had to hold the whole assemblage aloft like an Olympic torch.

I, along with a couple of curious neighbors, was impressed.

Doctor Sven held out the bouquet to me.

"This is just a token of our appreciation for being such a super patient," he announced. "How's the back?"

"Good, I replied. It's good, Doctor Sven." I took the bouquet and marveled. It looked like a tacky waterfall, exploding into color at the end of a cone-shaped handle.

"Don't let that thing touch the ground," Dr. Sven said.

"I won't, Doctor Sven."

"Gotta run now! Got many other super patients to visit!"

"Bye," I said, brandishing the streamers overhead as enthusiastically as I could.

"Ciao! And don't forget to fill out that comment card!" he said, shutting the doors to the Customer Appreciation Van.

"I won't, Doctor Sven."

"Super!"

Dr. Sven turned the key and the gleaming panels of the C.A.V. lit up with a bank of ruby lights.

He then revved the engine, which sounded as powerful as a small aircraft's primed for take-off. Indeed, as the van began to pull away, it was hard to resist the illusion that it was ascending.

As he waved back to me, Dr. Sven's final words were just audible:

"Don't forget to give us lots of 'Great's!!!"

CLICKERLAND

1

By 2062, the country had finally become a peaceable place to live. No more wars or terrorist threats. Everybody had friended everybody else. And the legislature had been replaced, for all practical purposes, with DEMOWEB.

Time after time, Congress hadn't polled well. Questions like, "Do you believe politicians respond to your personal needs?" or, "Would you like to see a smaller, more efficient government?" had ultimately sounded the death knell. There were representatives no longer, only Respondents ready to act upon data from DEMOWEB's consensus-modeling applications.

The Centerpol complex in New Jersey was the hub for popular initiatives. No one doubted the efficiency of the government's program, which enacted voter preferences at the touch of a button. If there was one thing those wizards at Centerpol knew how to do, it was design some killer software.

The president was also a populist choice. President Bieber was now an elderly man, but after twenty-four years in office, still looking good. And his numbers continued to trend upwards, or at least hold steady. This was despite the fact he wielded little more power than a prom king. In one Online Constitutional Convention after another, DEMOWEB users had voted to limit executive duties to posing with dignitaries and attending funerals of celebrities.

True, life expectancy wasn't quite what it was back in the day, probably because people demanded access to drugs and cures before they'd been proven effective. Compared to angels or crystals, the scientific method never received many *likes*. There was talk of universities paying researchers out of athletic budgets, but that was the kind of chitchat which circled the virtual drain and never reached the point of a voter referendum.

Sometimes folks began to sweat when prompted to a difficult vote by their handheld devices and yearned to flip ahead to view Results first. How could one possibly know whether or not to like something when other Friends' choices were hidden from view?

Fortunately, everyone knew you could slide a paperclip across one corner of the screen and it would flash ahead—for a split second. Long enough for a reassuring insight to dawn: "You know, that's pretty much the way I was going to vote, too."

2

Janey had always been a little off-center.

She was tantalized by the thought of straying off the grid. Maybe only a bit, or just for a while.

And she had qualms about instant tabulation. She knew she could get carried away at times and wasn't sure if it was the greatest thing for her initial preferences to become law. She would rather scroll through the endless Lobbylinks first, just to buy herself time to think.

It could be frustrating to see an issue go viral in an instant. Often, Janey flipped ahead to Vote Totals just to see if an election result was already a fait accompli.

Sometimes, if she saw a consensus only *beginning* to form in either direction, she entertained the thought of voting the opposite way, just to slow the DEMOWEB juggernaut down and give everyone out there a breather.

By the way—those handheld clickers were really, really spectacular and updated bimonthly. You could pick them up from a bin at any Wall2Wall and just key in your Social Stability number.

3

Janey worked at Wall2Wall, in the paint department.

Somewhere along the line, she must have *liked* art, or an art teacher, or simply updated her status while she was in art class. That was often the way that kind of thing found its way into one's profile. Before Janey entered high school, an interest in art became a fixed part of her identity.

At the Wall2Wall, Janey often found herself bored. But after all, it was a job, and they actually paid you to stand there while you texted. The part she liked best was mixing paints from swatches customers brought in until she had found a perfect match. Occasionally that could surprise you. You might find you needed, for example, a little green in the mix to get the red of a finish just right.

Once, playfully, Janey had splotched a little sunburst of acrylic paint around her plastic nametag.

This made most customers look twice, then shake their heads and smile.

Janey liked that, creating a tiny ripple effect.

4

She had met Bob at a nearby Display Storage Facility (DSF), which is what art galleries were called nowadays.

Most galleries had been rendered obsolete by virtual tours that seamlessly bridged museums across the globe. No need for lines or velvet ropes or security guards.

If you felt like having a guide, you could summon one of several different celebrity holograms or mute them—up to you.

Something appealed to Janey about the live experience she couldn't quite fathom.

A quiet feeling, empty and yet not.

5

The moment her field of vision crossed Bob's felt like a car crash.

From a bench, Janey had been scrutinizing a painting of two circles.

The two circumferences overlapped very slightly and in the middle ground was just a touch of brightness, or agitation.

It was certainly not in any way harmful, like staring at an eclipse, but somehow the whole experience unsettled her. She felt tears start to well up and averted her gaze.

Then Janey spotted Bob smiling at her. She smiled back.

It was the first emotional connection she'd made since she was a girl at school.

6

School, for most, was the true leveling influence. Those poor teachers had been reduced to freaks trying to put on a show for all the learning styles and learners—gesturing large and flitting around for the Visuals, talking in stage voices or blowing into kazoos for the Auditories, or pausing every now and then to let the Tactiles come up and have their feel.

When Janey thought back to her school days, she could remember a cavalcade of color and sound, but it was all very much like a slightly nauseating carnival ride. The only real constant had been the clickers.

Clickers allowed students instant input into what they were taught, how they were taught, and how much they wished to learn. In the lower grades, students were always mashing on the buttons just to watch the teacher contort like a marionette. In the upper grades, students flooded the devices with inane questions each morning just to keep the instructors off their back.

And so, what Janey recalled learning was: not much. No wonder she had trouble making up her mind!

Janey was the girl who held onto her stuffed animals just a bit later and dreamed distractedly out the classroom window just a bit longer or laughed at birthday parties just a little louder. And cried at sad movies, but didn't choose to click immediately on one of the alternate endings.

Against her parents' wishes, she had said enough is enough after high school, declining to pursue an ASD (Athletic Support Degree) in college, although she certainly had the tools for cheerleading. She also held off on setting up an account at ahoy.mate.com. There, based on your preferences, you were paired with someone of similar background, tastes, and physiognomy. The whole courtship thing was a snap.

Oh Janey, Janey.

At least she hadn't become an Outlier, openly rebelling against the government and earning herself a trip to Tokeville for some serious mainstreaming.

There, she might be found guilty without trial and forcibly dosed with Centrille, a new wonder drug that brought on sweet oblivion, making life float by on smooth strokes of an oar.

It also deleted one's mental profile permanently.

7

And so they met. They sat down and stared at the painting of the circles. They talked.

They toned down their clickers.

Bob monitored the gallery feed at the DSF and was a whiz at that kind of thing. He spent his time scooting around empty galleries on his Segway PT-1009 series, patrolling for art thieves who never came.

It was a job he found strangely exhilarating. In his best moments, he thought of himself as a composer, wending his way this way and that through bright paintings and sculptures and mixed-media productions.

Bob was not a tour guide, however, and certainly no art student—he just bounced along, from color to form to dissonance and back, like a big bumblebee in a sunny patch of clover.

Bob and Janey. Janey and Bob.

8

They began meeting when Janey was off work. The once-widely heralded architecture of this DSF facility, with its vast cylindrical corridors, comprised a strange and romantic setting after dark.

"What do you want to do?" Bob asked.

"Everything!" said Janey.

So they staged dinners in the sculpture garden and danced across the breezeways and made love like horny royals on the carpet beneath rich hanging tapestries.

They even dreamed of a life together off the grid.

So frightened were they of failing to be accounted for, however, that they got up every fifteen minutes or so to click *Not Sure* on the latest referendum.

In the dark ages before DEMOWEB, the Friend Networks had become so vast that they threatened to freeze everyone's system.

You might worry if you hadn't heard from that Friend of yours in Denver or Minneapolis who ordinarily posted hourly updates and start flooding his or her page. As a security measure to help regulate the flow of virtual traffic, the government had installed a Regional Vigilance in twelve hubs around the country. It soon became public information to know who was online at all times, or if any voters out there were neglecting their patriotic duty to make their voices heard.

Each hub was eventually subsumed by Centerpol, a strategic move to insure that citizens wouldn't trouble the government about every little thing.

A predator in Mrs. Smith's rose bushes or poorly bagged groceries might be cause for complaint, but didn't need to trigger a voter initiative.

On the other hand, if Mr. Smith suffered a stroke and was down for the count, the Emergency Messaging System would insure help was on the way. In a way, Centerpol was sort of like a Big Friend to all.

And when all was said and done, those new clickers truly *were* addictive.

On the strength of peer-reviewed studies on chimpanzees, Centerpol deemed it impossible for most people to forbear from checking inboxes every seventeen-and-a-half minutes, give or take.

If the Responders at Centerpol didn't hear from a person for a whole day, you could bet they would send out the cavalry.

9

It would have been hard for Janey to pinpoint just when she came up with the idea for the Big Showing.

She was now spending all (not *virtually* all) her spare time at the DSF, carrying on with Bob and examining paintings down to the last brushstroke. She began to reconstruct them in her mind's eye.

At the DSF, she had become a new person, glowing like a saint.

At work, she tried to tone it down, but wielded her employee discount with increasing éclat, purchasing so many cans of paint she started receiving text messages and coupons for home redecoration from her own branch.

Those discount offers became bigger and bigger as if luring her out to the edge of a consumer precipice.

Bob warned her to exercise caution. He had a justifiably modest opinion of his own intellect but didn't care to have anyone label him an Outlier and sauce him silly with any powerful drugs. Moreover, he didn't want to erase the new feeling he felt for Janey.

He now cared for her completely.

And he followed her around dutifully, setting up palettes and drip trays and trying to keep everything covered in plastic.

Janey called him a Big Ol' Worrywart.

Bob countered, calling Janey Some Kind of Daredevil.

They were in love, but Janey was also beginning to love something else, that feeling she got from totally losing herself in her work.

10

Swirls and splotches of color began to appear on the walls between paintings.

Despite Bob's warnings, Janey kept buying more paint. She used phony IDs or rang up cans as damaged merchandise and smuggled them out of the store.

Bob, when tasked, collected velvet rope and wire out of storage.

He also traveled for supplies to other DSFs, where he was waved to back rooms full of unused tools and electronics by apathetic guards who were clearly bored out of their skulls.

They said, just take all you want.

Bob knew tampering with the DEMOWEB network in any way was considered to be a truly seditious act, but by this point, Janey wasn't listening.

The Big Showing was afoot!

11

Janey had discovered a new sense of peace.

It was a feeling that didn't always last very long, and which some-times could be trailed by a little guilt. One didn't spend one's whole life on a social network without developing at least a little fellow-feeling for others.

Still, Janey managed to maintain her focus. What she really wanted, after all, was to share her work with Friends everywhere.

Then perhaps they could discover there was life off the grid, too.

12

Reluctantly, Bob set up his guy-wires and began powering up the DSF feed. The Big Showing was to be broadcast live.

He continued to grumble, warning Janey that those Vigilance troops didn't play around.

Janey tuned him out.

The two worked side by side, often in total silence.

Bob had long since assumed control of Janey's clicker.

These days she spent all her time up a ladder with trays of paint, so lost in her own world she would have missed answering the device even had it vibrated like Mount St. Helens.

13

By New Year's Eve, the Big Showing was all set to go down.

At the eleventh hour, Bob worked out the remaining kinks with the live feed and mounted the DSF webcam on a golf cart.

He and Janey then embraced for a long, long time before settling in for a once-in-a-lifetime ride.

"Let's go," Janey said.

And so they were off.

14

It looked and felt like a space launch.

Soft ropes hung along corridors like cords of a suspension bridge leading outward and upward.

Janey's bright borders trailed along the walls, then burst like comets.

An artwork appeared around each bend like a newly discovered star or planet.

The camera caught it all.

Fifteen seconds passed. Twenty.

Bob gave the golf cart a little more juice.

15

One minute. Two. Two and a half.

As it turns out, it was taking Centerpol Respondents a little longer to deal with hackers that night because several had been out celebrating New Year's and were a little tipsy and unsure just what they were seeing.

A countdown, a ball-drop, then a sort of trippy trip through a strange universe of shape and color?

It was all kind of transfixing.

But they shut down the feed.

16

The Vigilance troops, also groggier than usual, black helicoptered over from Jersey just minutes later.

"You are surrounded," they announced.

Duh, thought Janey and Bob.

"Surrender!" the officer in charge commanded, just for effect.

"Is that a carbine-action, five-kilo shot range laser rifle?" Bob asked appreciatively.

"Why, yes it is."

"With Google compassing, and that thing that freezes time?"

"Uh-huh."

Janey looked a little bored.

17

Afterwards, Janey and Bob were flown straight to a mainstreaming facility near Tokeville.

The next morning when their case number came up, they weren't interrogated or harassed.

Or even questioned very closely.

Instead, they were escorted by Vigilance troops into a hospital waiting room.

"Next in line," an elderly nurse barked.

Bob struggled, but it wasn't really necessary to be conscious to be dosed with Centrille. So one of the troops neatly clubbed him over the head when he tried to protect Janey.

From then on, it was smooth sailing.

Janey didn't resist at all. She was too busy composing another painting in her head, a beautiful work which no one but her would ever see.

She felt a pinprick in her arm and then her mental picture broke apart in a kaleidoscopic swirl.

She looked down at Bob, who was snoring near her feet with a big dumb smile.

She felt herself start to slide out of her chair, saw the swell of Bob's belly below, and smiled to herself because she knew it was going to be a soft landing.

III

A METHODICAL MADNESS

1

Sometimes when life begins to resemble art, you just want to run and hide.

Butch Jepson sat across from me on the La-Z-Boy, his teeth crunching pork rinds with grim determination. His pistol was out of its holster, set before him on the coffee table like fancy silverware. The TV provided the only light in the room, but the volume had been muted so we could listen to sounds coming from the night world outside my home in Flippen, Georgia. The sliding doors were open and a cool breeze blew through the screens. We were waiting, waiting.

On any other evening, I would have gotten up to fetch Butch a placemat so his weapon wouldn't scratch my table. But this was no ordinary occasion.

Behind the empty chairs on the patio deck—past the forlorn trampoline rusting in the fescue—beyond the line of shortleaf pines and dark shrubs, blinking with fireflies—there lurked an inhuman presence.

We were expecting an appearance of the Beast of Atlanta.

2

You feel bad for any A-level actor who can achieve fame and notoriety only by playing villains in B-level sci-fi and horror releases.

All the over-the-top, exaggerated expressions of the monster or villain make it difficult for a classically trained thespian to stretch his or her legs. Those legs are otherwise occupied trampling underlings or stalking human prey.

Eugene Sensa was something of an outlier in the entertainment trade. A method actor, no less, trained in the Strasberg school and later at the HB Studio with Uta Hagen, who at that point in her career still preached the controversial doctrine of "substitution"; i.e., the actor's need to realize a character by fusing certain aspects of his own identity with the part.

He was the son of the actor Sammy Sensa (formerly di Sensa), who had played popular police detective Joseph Mack on *City Streets*, a long-running TV cop show in the early 1960s.

Eugene's career had begun its downward spiral sometime in the 90s, when, past his prime as a leading man—even a despotic one—he had begun to take on roles requiring more make-up: evil space aliens, phantoms, and ghouls. He had a stagey voice that could really carry over farm fields or castle parapets and make the jowls of a rubber mask shake.

Eugene Sensa movies were rerun frequently on cable TV, and if you could abide all the commercial interruptions and hold your suspense through the break, they might even scare you.

Because he had started off playing serious stage roles that allowed him to bare his soul and further conditioned him as a method actor, you had to wonder about the disconnect between Eugene's early and late careers. What childhood secrets or traumatic episodes, if any, could possibly have provided him with a template for the sadists he had gone on to portray on screen?

It would be bizarre, indeed, if to flesh out his portrayals of famous characters like Vlad the Impaler, Cesare Borgia, or Boz Rippa the Robot King, in his mind Sensa was replaying a beating from a neighborhood bully or a singularly unpleasant dissection of a frog.

When I read in the *Atlanta Journal-Constitution* that a movie would be filmed in my area titled *Beast of Atlanta*, naturally I was curious. We don't often get that close to Hollywood down here. And when I saw the name Eugene Sensa linked to the production, I did a double-take, wondering if there was a "Jr." the editors had neglected to include.

The production featured a vengeful Green Man creature that emerges from a river hollow polluted by radioactive industrial waste.

I squinted again at the newspaper picture. Yes, that was Eugene all right, looking like an angry Greek god, wearing a headdress of twisted branches and a stony chest piece which made him appear slightly top-heavy.

3

I set out to interview Eugene Sensa while *Beast of Atlanta* was still in the preproduction stages.

The actor was gracious enough considering the fact he had spent two hours in make-up that day for a test fitting. It was seven a.m., and two make-up artists were already hard at work.

Eugene's skin had been tinted an ashen green-gray and his brow was extended to look more severe. A copious moustache and beard curled from his face akin to those found on Roman sculptures of Pan. Leaves sprouted amid the hair to make him look even wilder and surlier.

Later, when a headpiece of spiked branches and thorns were affixed, along with a hard carapace of stone armor bulging with faux muscle definition, the illusion of a living tree-man who had ripped himself from the earth to seek terrible vengeance would be almost complete.

The last touch, I learned, would be a fitting in the prop department with two prosthetic pieces. These would extend Eugene's arms like long branches and terminate in sharp, retractable claws.

I asked Eugene Sensa whether all the hours in make-up were a bother. "No."

"Is it hard to connect with a character that is a supernatural being?"
"Not at all," he answered.

I wondered if the earliness of the hour rendered him laconic, or whether the foundation applied to the corners of his mouth simply made it difficult for him to speak.

But then Eugene elaborated. "The Green Man is an old belief," he said, "a god-like being who is all about protecting the forest. Anyone who considers himself an environmentalist can surely find something to admire in that."

"But is it possible to fully realize such a character from the inside out?" I asked. "You're a method actor by training, aren't you, or has that changed over the years?"

"Acting never changes for me," he said. "It's what I do. I may be in make-up every morning, but I will always use that time to prepare and step into a role."

"That's interesting," I said. "That sense of craft you bring to a role has always given you a great edge over other horror movie actors, those who think just prancing around in a gruesome costume is enough . . . ."

Eugene held up a hand as if he had already heard enough of my question.

"A costume is only a *means*," he said. "It gives one a tool for expressing inner feelings—in this case, a kind of primal rage."

"That's what interests me," I said. "How does one tap into a character like the Green Man? Whip oneself into a homicidal frenzy?"

"You have it backwards," he said. "I don't tap into 'the Green Man' at all. I tap into myself, and thereby *become* the Green Man."

To me, this reply seemed just a tad glib. So I tried a slight change of focus.

"You grew up in Hollywood, right? Sammy Sensa's son?"

"That's right."

"Did you have a love of nature as a boy? Did you spend a lot of time in the Sierras, for example?"

"I took a field trip there once for school, I believe," Eugene answered. "But my education was mostly accomplished with tutors. My mother left the family when I was just a boy," he added. "So my brother and I spent most days on the set with Pops."

I searched my memory for what I could recall of Sammy Sensa, drawing mostly a blank.

The image Sammy had always projected on *City Streets* was that of a no-nonsense tough guy-cum-detective; hardly your family man.

"Sammy Sensa must have been kind of a demanding father," I reflected, thinking aloud. "I imagine he kept a pretty tight rein on you and your brother—er, what's his name?"

"My brother's name was Franklin," Eugene replied, coolly. "He died of a drug overdose as a teenager."

"Oh, I'm sorry," I said.

The conversation stalled there for a moment.

I knew our time together must be winding down, too, because Eugene's personal assistant, a local theater student named Justin Badcock, came out and whispered something in his ear.

Justin was a former standout offensive lineman in high school who had banged up a knee and later decided to drop football to pursue an acting career.

In the remaining seconds of the interview, I decided to attempt a Hail Mary pass of my own, hoping to glean whatever nugget of final wisdom I could from my subject.

"So, how do you do it, Eugene? How can you search inside yourself to become the Green Man?"

"I'm an *actor*," he declaimed.

4

Beast of Atlanta would have flown by under the radar but for a pair of unfortunate occurrences.

The first transpired when the production was still in preproduction. While clearing an area for shooting in some thick woods along the Chattahoochee, the location crew discovered the body of a jogger missing for several weeks.

Despite the obvious lack of any connection to the film shoot, the fact that a corpse had been found covered in scratches near the set of a monster flick was just too good for the press to leave alone. It was an easy cover story that got picked up and broadcast on all the local networks.

Then, in response to an off-the-wall question at a press conference, the Atlanta Chief of Police tried to reassure reporters the attacker had been human, not an animal, despite the fact that the body showed signs of having been mauled more recently.

His remark set off another firestorm.

When I returned to the set, Eugene was sequestered in his trailer amid all the ado. But I spied Justin Badcock making a surreptitious trip back from craft service bearing an herbal tea.

"Hey. How's Eugene taking all this?"

"He's holding up," Justin said, with a trace of real affection in his voice. "He's a perfessional."

"He's training me to be an actor, too, you know," Justin added.

"That's great," I said, encouragingly. "You've really got an opportunity to learn from someone whose teachers and teachers' teachers were the best."

"I know that!" he retorted.

"So, what's he teaching you?" I asked, as though soliciting an answer from one of my own students.

"To . . . to live the part, I guess. To become another person . . . walk around in someone else's skin."

Then Justin remembered his errand, telling me Eugene was impatiently waiting for his tea.

"Were you the one who discovered the body?" I asked him, really only to make conversation.

"Nope," he replied, scowling. "Why did you say that?"

"No reason."

5

The discovery of the mauled body resulted in heightened security on the set, if for no other reason than the press had fallen in love with the story and grew intrigued when Eugene Sensa refused to grant interviews.

About this time, I made the acquaintance of Butch Jepson.

Butch once completed the sixty-one day course to become Ranger-qualified at the RTB Ranger School at Fort Benning, Georgia. But shortly afterwards, he received a medical discharge from the Army for an asthma condition. He had been recently been hired as an extra security guard through a local agency which came cheap and promised discretion.

Although no more than thirty, Butch was stocky and balding, one of those men who looked ten years older than his age. Part of that dying Southern breed that sometimes spit before they talked, just to cleanse the palate.

Butch didn't care much for the Hollywood types he had been assigned to babysit but took to me just fine when he found out we were near neighbors. He had an abiding love for Henry County. I heard him moan that the big-city crime from Atlanta was slowly descending upon us.

This being the age of Google, I also continued my research into Eugene Sensa and his father.

They had clearly been opposites. Sammy Sensa told reporters often enough how acting was just another job to him, a paycheck—something much like his character Detective Joe Mack might say, or did say.

There were no references in the online archives to Sammy's former wife. Sammy had apparently encouraged the myth that he was a widower left to raise his two boys. When in fact, his wife had divorced him and there were guarded references to his past problems with alcoholism and the turmoil it had caused his family. Still, Sammy had happily remarried in his sixties, when both of his boys would have been grown, and afterwards he more or less retired from acting. He died in 2002.

Fan sites can create interference for background searches and make it difficult to locate unbiased biographical details. But one story I ran across interested me, and seemed genuine—a report of an allegation of abuse against Sammy Sensa concerning two unnamed children. Apparently, the juveniles had created some disturbance near the set and Sammy borrowed keys from his producer to lock them in a jail cell as a punishment. He left the poor kids there in darkness overnight. When discovered the following morning, they were in sad shape.

Charges were never filed, and the newspapers never revealed the identity of the two boys. But I had a hunch their names might have been Eugene and Franklin.

I knew it would be quite difficult to gain access to Eugene Sensa again to ask him about this incident, especially now that filming had begun and he was growing daily into his Green Man character. On top of this, he had a former high school all-American candidate escorting him at all times around the set and blocking the entrance to his trailer.

But there couldn't be any harm just in asking him a question, right?

6

When a second body was found near the set of *Beast of Atlanta*, the movie production quickly became national news.

This was the corpse of a homeless man who died in the South Fulton neighborhood where the crew was filming, one known to be a frequent haunt of drug dealers and gangs. To a cinematographer's eye, it had just the right look for a scene of the Green Man marching into town.

The second victim had died of exposure. To the press, however, the more telling detail was the condition of the body. Like the jogger at the park, it looked as though it had been raked over by claws.

Hearing the news report on the radio, I decided to call up my new friend Butch to ask him how things were going on the set.

Miserable but grateful for someone to talk to, he decided to give me an earful.

The producers had issued Eugene Sensa an ultimatum, insisting that he do his part to allay further rumors by coming out of his trailer to release a statement. It was only a monster flick, after all. They saw no reason their actor had to train in there like DeNiro for *Raging Bull*.

Wrong argument to use on Eugene.

He proceeded to throw a tantrum on set, turning over lighting screens and an equipment stand. And all in front of a group of reporters, no less, providing them with plenty of copy about the Beast of Atlanta behaving like the Beast of Atlanta.

"I think this Sensa guy's hiding something, M.V.," Butch muttered to me over the phone.

I asked Butch what he meant.

"I mean, there's this corpse what was found just a few blocks from his trailer, right, and the guy's acting real crazy."

"Are you suggesting he had anything to do with it?"

There was a pause, and I thought I heard the sound of Butch spitting on the ground.

"Don't know, M.V., I'm just sayin'.

"It's like, he's above everybody else and can't be interrupted by no one no more, even when he's not on the set. Drop by and see for yourself."

"I think I just might."

7

I mulled over Butch's theory while driving into the city. Had the fading Hollywood star, Eugene Sensa, truly lost his grip? Was he so intent on fusing his identity with his character's that he'd literally turned homicidal?

As soon as I arrived, I could see the mood at the shoot had changed dramatically. The producers, tiring of Eugene's demands, had retaliated by opening the set to the press. Eugene, finally yielding under pressure, reluctantly agreed to throw reporters a bone.

They were lined up outside his trailer right now, no doubt hoping for another meltdown.

After a moderate wait, Eugene emerged from the trailer wearing full beard and make-up but without the foliate head dress or frowning eyebrows.

Instead of appearing angry or vengeful, he actually was looking today like one of the more grandfatherly gods in the pantheon.

He raised his hand for quiet.

"I don't have much to say on the subject of the bodies, gentlemen and ladies, other than that it's been a truly sad and tragic sequence of events, and my heart goes out to the families of the victims.

"I do not follow news reports as closely as perhaps I should while I am at work, but I have been filled in on the details, which I find most distressing.

"Certainly, when these real-life tragedies occur, they must serve as a reminder to us all of how short and precious life can be."

The questions ensued, mostly concerning his role in the film.

Eugene began to warm to his audience. Eventually, when one woman asked about his recent outburst on set, he did about as good an impression of sheepishness as I have ever seen.

Eugene cast his eyes down and confided, abashedly, that perhaps he had inherited a little of the tough cop from his Italian father.

This drew appreciative murmurs from some of our more star-struck local reporters, who generally warm at the mention of any celebrity.

A couple of softball questions followed concerning *City Streets*, and Eugene subtly managed to slip in there, somehow, the fact that it had been almost ten years to the day since he'd visited his father on his deathbed.

More sympathetic murmurs.

Justin Badcock finally stepped forward to signal that the question-and-answer period was over.

Before any reporters could protest, Eugene announced, "I'm afraid duty calls, gentlemen and ladies."

"As Joe Mack would say, a man has to go out there and do the best job he can to make a buck," he added.

"I have sincerely enjoyed our time together. Thank you!"

Then he ducked back into the trailer, waving.

About forty minutes later, all the reporters had left peacefully without needing any prompting from Butch.

My security guard friend was looking somewhat miserable following Eugene's performance.

"I tell you, he was acting crazy, M.V!"

I told Butch I believed him. And I did, sort of.

But it also appeared to me that Eugene's on/off switch was fully operational; a few weeks of pouncing upon industrialists and innocent bystanders and pretending to rip them apart had not permanently altered his brain.

Another half hour passed.

Then Justin Badcock, leading Eugene, emerged from the trailer en route to make-up.

Although Justin reflexively attempted to block my approach, I greeted Eugene and complimented him on his handling of the press conference.

The actor didn't respond.

Unsure if his boss was still in public address mode, Justin stepped to one side.

I found myself looking into the eyes of something inhuman.

Eugene wore red contact lenses which were frightening in the sunlight. He still had not donned his prosthetic arms, but that hardly mattered. He was now a vengeful god: the Green Man.

The creature snarled.

I was taken aback by Eugene Sensa's complete immersion in character. But after a beat or two, I thought I might as well try probing behind the mask.

So I asked Eugene a question I had prepared carefully—a question about a single father, his two little boys, and a jail cell somewhere in West Covina.

What happened next was a quick blur.

Its face contorting with genuine rage, the Beast lunged forward and began tearing at me, savagely but harmlessly, sans stage claws.

Justin and Butch lunged forward immediately to separate us, bumping bellies. The force of their impact sent everybody reeling.

"I'll kill that scribbler!" rasped Eugene, in his deep voice.

Justin hugged his mentor in his powerful arms and steered him back towards make-up.

Wisely, Butch stepped aside to let both pass. Then he looked at me with just a trace of a smile.

"Told you so," he muttered.

8

Later Butch called me, possibly just to rub it in further.

Apparently, after two full hours of shooting that day, Eugene Sensa had returned to his trailer still furious, speaking to no one, not even to Justin.

"They say he was a real monster on the set, too," Butch joked.

Then Butch assumed a professional tone—asking me if, in my opinion, the man had been only acting earlier.

"I think it's precisely when Eugene Sensa's acting that he becomes the most dangerous," I offered. "That's when his switch gets stuck, and when he has trouble turning it off."

"Well, just a heads-up, then," Butch replied. "I told Justin I had some questions about his boss' little performance this afternoon and to let me know just as soon as he got back to make-up."

"So?"

"So Mr. Sensa never reported to make-up! And his whereabouts, at this time, are unknown. Justin's out looking for him."

"Anyway, be on your guard," he added.

"You're not actually serious? The Beast of Atlanta might be headed my way?"

"Just keep your doors locked, as a precaution, and call me if you notice anything unusual. I'll keep you posted . . . neighbor."

"Thanks," I said.

9

The first phone call came about an hour later.

I felt relieved to hear the ring, thinking Butch was calling me back with good news about Eugene's return.

When I picked up the phone, however, the line went dead.

I considered punching in Butch's number but held off, thinking he might have lost the signal on his end and would try me back.

The phone rang a second time, and then stopped.

This time, I checked the caller ID—an unknown number. So I promptly called Butch.

"Butch Jepson," he answered.

"You been calling me up, Butch?"

"Nope," he replied. "Whassup?"

I told him about the second hang-up.

He told me to sit tight, he wasn't doing much of anything and might as well drop on by.

No need for alarm, but Eugene and Justin were still nowhere to be found.

10

And so here we are again—me on the sofa and Butch half-reclining on the chair.

We haven't talked much. To regale me, Butch has hooked his small camera up to my TV and has been playing back a couple of video clips taken during the day's filming.

"Here's my favorite part, right he-ah," he says, pausing over a shot of the Green Man tearing into two picnickers.

"Watch it again?" he asks, mischievously.

"Pass."

11

Outside the window, the pines grow darker minute by minute.

Butch assures me a noise I hear is probably just the clatter of wind chimes but squeaks his chair into the upright position and starts to grope for his gun.

Next I am certain that I see a black shadow crawl past the sliding doors.

We wait in silence, Butch with gun in left hand pointed toward any oncoming threat and me sitting off-center on the couch.

We are frozen in this tableau for a while.

Butch starts to grow restless, his thick leg twitching up and down.

Finally, he whispers he is going to go out to make a sweep of the yard and to just sit tight.

I-have-no-problem-with-that, I whisper back.

12

Somewhere out in the darkness, Butch is groping along.

He has let himself out the front door and crept around back. For a heavyset man, he is capable of delicate movement.

I am under his strict instructions not to hit the outdoor floodlights unless and until he gives me a shout. So I wait by the back porch switch.

I hear nothing for the first thirty seconds.

Nothing for another fifteen.

Then all at once, the sounds of a scuffle.

Butch yells, *"Now!"*

I hit the lights.

Out in the yard stands the frightening figure of what appears to be a half-man, half-stag. Its long, branchlike claws are poised over Butch's body.

Butch's right shirt arm has been torn into neat shreds. In the deep background, against the line of pines, looms a taller, blacker figure.

Viciously, the Beast of Atlanta swipes at Butch again.

Butch raises his wounded arm to ward off the blow.

The Beast's sharp claws neatly sever two of Butch's fingers.

The security guard does not respond verbally. Instead, he angrily swings his uninjured fist around. The pistol he holds connects with the monster's jawbone.

The Beast takes a half step back, then roars in fury and closes in again. With its heavy muscles, stony armor and wicked claws, it looks invincible.

Butch lowers his gun and calmly shoots the Beast in the shoulder, shattering the faux chest carapace.

This time, the creature falls to the ground.

Running out the door, I yell, "Look out!"

Too late—the looming black figure sails into the foreground, knocking the security guard down.

The two wrestle briefly on the ground. Then both stand up and trade somewhat awkward blows.

Butch deftly slips behind the assailant and applies his bloody fist to the man's throat in a Ranger chokehold. That paralyzes him.

The Beast of Atlanta, however, is not dead. It has only been winded by the bullet to its chest armor, which now looks as cracked as the shell of a road-killed turtle. The hard fall to the ground has also snapped some of the branches surrounding its head.

Exhausted, the creature makes one more feeble effort to rise, but now seems confused and uncertain of purpose, like an actor unused to improv.

Yes, very like an actor.

I walk over and gently but firmly place my foot on Eugene Sensa's chest, pushing him down onto the grass.

"Cut!" I say, not trying at all to be funny.

13

Beast of Atlanta opened to solid reviews. The fact that it ultimately turned out to be actor Eugene Sensa's swansong gave it a morbid mystique and still makes it a fan favorite.

Eugene had to be hospitalized before completion of the filming for heat prostration and dehydration. He never returned to the set. To finish the picture, the studio had to call in the actor Ron Perlman, who quickly polished off Eugene Sensa's remaining scenes—quite ably, I might add.

The details surrounding the end of the shoot were successfully kept out of the press. Part of the subsequent PR campaign was engineered to sell the public the idea Eugene's unfortunate departure was part of a series of unfortunate events and unsolved crimes that had jinxed the production from the onset, nearly derailing it.

Justin Badcock was arrested and released. He had found Eugene along the roadway and only managed to get his mentor into the car with a promise to take him anywhere he wished to go, no questions asked.

Although Eugene was having some major issues with his on/off switch by that point, the effect of wearing the costume in the Georgia heat and humidity may have been what ultimately pushed him over the edge.

Justin has since reconsidered his plans for an acting career and is once again playing football for a Division I school.

Butch Jepson collected a nice cash settlement from the studio after signing a contract with a written proviso stating that his continued discretion regarding the unfortunate circumstances surrounding the filming would be greatly appreciated and expected.

Despite his newfound wealth, Butch was never tempted to move out of the county. I saw him recently at our local Golden Corral. He was wearing a parrot shirt that must have been a 4x-Large, and which made him look like a parachutist who had just crash-landed.

Butch waved to me. The fingers on his hand were neatly reattached, leaving no visible scars.

I watched as he passed through the line working the crowd, nodding and smiling to his fellow Henry Countians. Really, you couldn't picture a man looking more content with himself.

And why not? Not every guy gets the chance to face down a monster.

AN UNKNOWN QUANTITY

1

"Really, Dr. M., this guy's not human."

"He's some kind of alien!"

"Please. Not all at once."

I don't recommend anyone try holding a speaker-phone conversation with three excitable film students at the same time. Often, it's one step forward and two steps back.

"Let me talk to Brianna One, first."

"I'm here."

"What exactly did you see?"

"Dr. Dula pulled out a gun—it looked like a Martian ray gun or something. He aimed it at a chair and this ray of light shot out, kind of like a laser pointer. Then the chair floated up in the air!"

"Hmmm. You *are* aware that he is in charge of special effects?"

"This wasn't a special effect! We're not stupid."

Ah. That would be Brianna Two.

"No one's calling anyone stupid," I said. "But you know, it might have been a special chair filled with hydrogen gas or something. Maybe the laser pointer device just activated a switch."

"Then he pointed the gun at Brandon. He threatened to send him straight into space, too, if we didn't stop meddling with his stuff."

"Sounds like he might have had a point. There are a lot of expensive gadgets in a studio prop area, you know—smoke bombs, incendiary devices, guns which can misfire. You guys were supposed to be interning in the Art Department. Maybe you'd better stay put."

"Is Brandon there, too?" I asked.

"Yep."

"Brandon, you OK?"

"Yep."

"Maybe you can explain to me why Brianna One and Brianna Two think my friend Dr. Haile Dula is an alien."

"Well, he is kind of weird looking. He has this bulb-shaped head and big eyes. And he acts so spaced-out, like he's on some kind of helium high."

In the background, someone giggled. I recognized this as Brianna One.

I sighed. And this was a generation of kids raised on multiculturalism? Why would they jump to the conclusion this poor man was an alien, versus, say, a magician or even a wizard? Don't they call them "special effects wizards"?

2

When I actually put this suggestion to Brianna Two the next day, she rolled her eyes with that ironic look meant to communicate, "I'm *sure!*"

"*Really*, Dr. M.?" she protested. "I outgrew Harry Potter a long time ago."

She and her friends apparently placed wizards and aliens in two separate categories, both of which defied critical thinking. In Brianna Two's mind, alien encounters had been "documented" everywhere on the Internet; and more importantly, had the appeal of advanced technology on their side. Science was simply an unknown quantity for some of these students—they had skipped the more intellectually curious Bill Nye the Science Guy or Beakman childhood phases that might have inspired them to become inventors themselves, settling for becoming more prolific users of new devices. They carried iPhones and tablets and were true believers in the power of the Net to counsel them in their consumer choices, guide them to their destination, or to help them make new friends.

In this case, however, the complaints of the Briannas and Brandon had to be taken seriously. I didn't want parents calling the university complaining that a man had pointed a gun at their child's head while on a school-sponsored internship and the institution had done nothing to address the situation.

And in truth, I had met Dr. Haile Dula only once at a party at my director friend Evan's house, and thus couldn't vouch very confidently for his character—nor stake my tenure on it. As I recall, our conversation mainly concerned Ethio Jazz. Originally from Addis Ababa, Dula graduated from MIT as an astrophysicist and later became a research scientist for a Japanese aerospace company that manufactured navigation systems and heavily invested in the movie industry.

Given his background, Dr. Dula was occasionally, and no doubt reluctantly, pressed into service as a special effects consultant. This pure scientist had been introduced to me as an "unqualified genius" by Evan, although that didn't necessarily mean a lot, coming from Evan.

All things considered, I decided it would be a wise thing to drop by the set that evening after I had dismissed my class.

3

The shoot was over for the day when I arrived at the J.A. Waldrus, Jr. Memorial Observatory in Vinings.

The movie title sounded innocent enough, to me: *Flubberology 101*. It conjured up a rather pleasant image of Fred MacMurray puttering around his lab as the Absent–Minded Professor.

I caught a production assistant coming out the door and asked her where I might find Dr. Dula. She directed me toward the planetarium.

There, I encountered heavy doors designed to block out light. They were closed but unlocked, and so, after getting no response to my knock, I entered.

What I discovered was a simply astounding set. Under a giant dome, objects were suspended in mid-air—a sofa, chairs, a big screen TV with a dangling cord, a wooden table, heavy textbooks; and, toward the top of the domed ceiling—where the waning sun just barely shone through—a potted palm tree, some bric-a-brac, and a smiling bust of Albert Einstein.

Dr. Dula stood on a stepladder toward the far wall. He was reaching up with a long pool net, trying to pull some of the props back down. He was quite a short man, so while the pole must have been ten feet long, its reach was nowhere near long enough for the net to achieve this purpose.

"What's up?" I asked, not consciously intending a pun.

"I am having difficulties with this phase," Dr. Dula said. "I can beam them up, but then you have to try to weight them down."

"Ah," I said. "This is precisely the sort of task you should put my interns to work on, Haile. I think they need to learn there's a lot of sweat behind the scenes in show biz; that it's not all bright lights and glitter."

"This is science, not show business," Dula snapped back.

"No offense," I replied.

He didn't respond.

"So, this armchair is some kind of inflatable, right?" I queried, stroking a cushion just overhead.

I was impressed. The chair felt just as plush as the real thing. If you dozed off on it, drifting in space, my god you'd sleep well!

"No," he said. "Just stripped of gravitons."

Now I was taken aback.

"How is that possible?" I asked.

"Maybe you'd better leave now," he said.

"Look, Haile, I'm not here *entirely* to pay you a social call," I said, adjusting my tone a little.

"I'm sorry to say I received a complaint from one of my interns today—that you pointed a prop gun at someone."

That got no response from him, either.

"I'm afraid that's simply not the kind of joke that will fly in this country post 9/11," I continued, suddenly wondering to myself, apropos of nothing in particular, whether Dr. Dula technically was a resident alien.

"The Higgs-boson Neutralizer is not a joke," he said, now defensive, hopping down from his stepladder.

Then, more obligingly: "Would you like to see it?"

"Sure," I replied, curious.

From a cabinet, Dula pulled out a gun exactly like Brianna One had described. It had a puffy central chamber and a bright blue nozzle at one end. Deftly, he then stooped to attach his new Higgs-boson Neutralizer to a power generator, rather like a dentist's drill.

With a strange, nerdish giggle, he aimed the device at me.

"Hey," I told him. "Easy!"

"I've been meaning to try it out on humans," he said, matter-offactly. Then, just as casually, he swung the gun over to a nearby camera crane.

I watched as a beam of light shot out and hit the heavy crane, point blank. Briefly, a soft red penumbra appeared around it, and then a faint film of condensation or precipitate.

Sure enough, the camera crane began to quiver.

And then, separating from it base, it rose upward to take its place alongside the other flotsam.

"It's lighter than air!" Dula gleefully exclaimed.

He zapped the camera crane again, and again, until it climbed more rapidly, crashing a hole through the glass ceiling of the observatory.

"I'm sorry. I can't help myself sometimes," he said.

I ducked a shower of minute shards.

"I think I'll be off now," I said.

"The H.B.N. is top secret," he said, suddenly suspicious. "How do I know you won't tell, like those annoying kids I caught spying? All of them with the same name, too, like some particularly pernicious order of biota."

He pointed the gun at me again.

"Funny," I said, trying to pass the whole situation off as a joke. "They thought you were an alien species, too."

That distracted him just enough.

I lunged forward, attempting to wrest the weapon from Dula's smallish hand.

At the same time, a light ray shot out and hit him squarely in the middle of the forehead.

I saw the soft red outline appear around his face, and his eyebrows appeared a frosty white. In that moment, he really did look like some sort of extraterrestrial.

Strangely, however, Dr. Haile Dula didn't seem to mind this sudden turn of events. In fact, he was quite giddily elated.

He chuckled as he started to float toward the domed ceiling. "It works! It works!" he chortled, happy as a child.

For some reason, instead of hightailing it out of there, I began to feel sorry for this little man—a lonely, bona fide genius. He had truly been a stranger in a strange land.

I picked up the pool net and raised it to him.

"Here," I said, in as gentle a tone as possible. "Just grab the end, Haile, and then we'll sit down together and discuss this situation like colleagues."

"Never!" he said, pushing the net aside.

Before I could plot my next move, Dula raised the gun once more.

But this time, he trained the weapon on himself.

"I am tired of all you people, your ignorance and your shallow political correctness!"

The Higgs-boson Neutralizer hummed again.

A darker red aura lit up around his face. The scientist rose with a jerk to the ceiling as the power cable, still attached to the H.B.N. device, lost all of its slack with a loud whip. The cord immediately strained to the breaking point.

And then I gazed, open mouthed, as it snapped, and Dr. Haile Dula rocketed through the hole in the roof, still holding onto his prize invention.

The useless power cable thumped heavily to the floor.

For a few seconds, I tried to track Dr. Dula's trajectory through the dome of the observatory.

I could follow the glint of his white lab coat against the evening sky, now overcast with dark clouds.

The white glint shot upward in a steep parabolic arc and grew smaller and smaller until it finally vanished into space.

Into the unknown.

THE LYCAN, THE WITCH, AND THE WARDROBE

1

For those who've never had the experience of climbing Stone Mountain in Georgia, the place is about as close to being on the moon as one can imagine. The barren surface of the white granite outcrop is worn smooth and pitted with craters and loose stone. To complete the lunar illusion, you can crouch low and screen out the sparsely scattered shrubs and trees that appear to defy all odds for survival by growing straight out of solid rock. That is, if you can get there before the hordes of hikers arrive.

It naturally occurred to me to recommend Stone Mountain as a locale when Raven Ripley came to my office pitching her idea for a student film project, one which required extensive shots of a moonscape.

She instantly took to the idea. A transfer student from New Jersey, she knew very little about our local area.

Raven's film did not strike me at the time as a particularly ambitious one, at least not for an honor student. It all sounded rather pulpy, a story of an astronaut-werewolf who suppresses his bestial side for years but then starts to melt down after his spacecraft crash-lands on an alien moon. The working title was *Moonwrecked!*

Er—I'm punching up that premise a bit. Raven was one of my better students, a fan of Marguerite Duras and Simone de Beauvoir, but she had come into my office that day with only a mass of scribbled notes.

2

She had also brought along with her another student, Denilson Gobo.

Denilson was a genial and well-liked junior from Brazil who offset his limited English skills by smiling a lot and inviting his tongue-tied American peers to call him "Denny." He seemed quite comfortable occupying the bottom of the curve in my film class, too, as though doing so fulfilled his sense of camaraderie with the other students. He had come to the university to play soccer, and soccer just about summed him up.

I briefly wondered why Raven had chosen to share her project with Denilson Gobo, but perhaps the answer was right there in front of me. Denilson wore a black V-neck Adidas warm-up shirt that nicely framed his muscled chest. With his neatly trimmed ball of black hair, dark eyebrows, and full lips, he was the spitting image of the teen heartthrob Taylor Lautner.

"So, this guy's your leading man, huh?"

"Yeah. I'm totally on Team Denny," Raven said.

"And you just know the audience will go for him, too," she added, reaching over and stroking his glossy shirt.

Perhaps Raven has a crush, I speculated, although I knew she had actively volunteered for the film series sponsored by our GLBT Club that spring. I am faculty advisor to this club, which generally can use all the support it can get in the Deep South.

"You think you can get a strong acting performance out of him? Denilson, can you do primal rage?"

Denilson smiled widely, showing a camera-ready set of white teeth.

"Huh," I said. "That reminds me, I really ought to see a dentist."

"So what are you going to use for the astronaut suits?" I asked Raven, changing the subject.

"I'm going to improvise," Raven said. "We have some beekeeper outfits, and we can top them off with motorcycle helmets or something."

"Well, let's take a look at this treatment of yours," I said, reaching out for the sheaf of pages she had brought in.

3

The first thing that struck me about the carelessly scribbled treatment was that Raven's werewolf-astronaut doesn't display any shaggy 'do or elongated canines until well after the crash-landing. Then he becomes pure wolf, tearing out of his space suit to reveal his manly chest in the style of one of those awful teenage bodice-rippers.

"Ah—how come this werewolf doesn't lose it sooner?"

"He's really more of a *lycan* than a werewolf," Raven answered. "It's always been there in his nature to transform, but he's been in psychotherapy and heavily dosed with medication to control his urges. He's also a military pilot, schooled to keep his cool. As long as he attacks only enemies he can't see, he's OK."

"That's a nice duality," I commented, although I got the impression Raven might have been making all this up on the spot. She was a smart one.

"But if he goes from being conflicted to going completely lobo— sorry—isn't that a step down? Is there a point?"

I looked over at Denilson as though looking for confirmation. His face was a complete blank.

"He's free," Raven said. "That's the point."

"I wasn't so much looking to make a *genre* pic," she added.

"I see. So we don't need to worry about the fact he's suddenly a wolf with no place to go."

She shrugged.

"Any love interest?" I wondered.

"Kinda," Raven Ripley said, her green eyes glittering a little. "His co-pilot on the mission is a female he's attracted to, but knows he can't have. Her marriage and conventional morals won't permit that."

"Who's playing her?" I asked, knowing that most of the other students in the class would be preoccupied with their own final projects.

"My roommate," Raven replied, with perhaps just a hint in her voice of either envy or resentment.

"So does he infect her and make her his moon-maid? Do they abandon the mission and run off along the craters together?"

"Don't make me gag," Raven said.

"So what, then?"

"He bites off her stupid, annoying head."

Denilson just nodded, as though this sort of thing would be no problem for him.

Raven clearly had him on board with her project, and why not? Working with one of the best students for a change would be a golden opportunity for him to raise his grade and keep Coach Carlson happy, too.

"All right," I said. "Green light!"

4

Please understand—I don't usually get involved in student projects past the point of the shooting script.

But in this case, since I had suggested the Stone Mountain locale myself, I felt somewhat responsible for any events that might transpire on the set.

I knew some of the outcroppings supported very fragile ecosystems; hence it would be important to keep the small production small. It also happened that a neighbor of mine, a docent at the park, had arranged personally for Raven Ripley to film there one weeknight just after close. So naturally, I felt obliged to observe.

Raven's crew, consisting of Denilson and four other soccer players, had hauled up all the gear and props along an access road earlier that afternoon.

For the past two hours, Raven had shot some establishing footage of the mountaintop and of the astronauts crawling out of the wreckage in their scorched white beekeeper outfits.

In preparation for Denilson's wardrobe-ripping scene, her tripod was now wedged into a crack overlooking a large crater.

All throughout these preliminaries, Jenna Higgs had been a real trouper, I thought.

This, despite the fact there was obvious tension on the set between herself and the director.

I noticed Raven never looked directly at Jenna when she gave an instruction; and even then, only referred to her roommate as "She" or "Lana," her character name. But Jenna never questioned Raven's directorial prerogative, perhaps because she was too polite, or perhaps because she wanted to preserve her opportunity to be a leading lady.

I was amused by her. She was every bit Raven's opposite. A central Georgia native, religious studies major, and accomplished cross-country runner, she was surely as white bread as Raven was rye.

With such palpable tension on the set, it was not hard to see how there could have been a war of wills between the two. And the tension only grew stronger when Raven took Denilson aside for an hour, never once speaking to Jenna.

"What is she *doing?*" Jenna finally asked, of no one in particular.

I thought I had better keep her company for a while.

"Denilson may need a little extra coaching for this scene," I suggested, to reassure her. "Up till this point in time, he's really just had to be himself, rescuing a lady and performing a few athletic maneuvers. Now he has to stop being Mr. Nice Guy and become a monster."

"Oooh. Creepy!"

"You're doing just fine, though, you know."

"Really, professor?" Jenna replied, beaming.

She certainly had more than enough charisma for a leading lady.

"Well, you know, back in high school, we performed *Singin' in the Rain*. I played Lina Lamont, and it was such a great experience—of course it was just a little ole school, but everyone said I did a fabulous job."

"I believe it. You seem like a natural."

"But this is my first-ever film role, and I'm kind of stressed because I'm just not sure what I'm supposed to be doing, or what my character is really trying to accomplish in this scene—I really wish I had more of a clue."

"I'm sure Raven will drop by soon to give you a little coaching, too."

"Oh. *Her*," Jenna said, and then fell silent.

5

After another forty-five minutes passed and still no appearance from Raven, I couldn't help but share some of Jenna Higgs' growing anxiety.

After all, this would be the climactic scene in the film for her, too, and Raven had absented herself for nearly two hours. The soccer guys had gone off to explore and I was starting to feel more and more like a chaperone.

Jenna and I sat on two rocks near a stunted pine tree. I asked her how she and Raven got along as roommates, and she took this as her cue to do a little venting.

"You know, I try to turn the other cheek, but it's hard sometimes. The lesbian thing doesn't bother me—it's her own lifestyle choice, I guess. But I let her know very clearly I wasn't interested in her *that* way.

"For a while, you know, I thought she might be obsessed with me. One time I found these Popsicle sticks around my bed. I asked Raven what they were for, and she tried to act all innocent, like they wasn't even hers. Maybe she was just trying to be funny. I don't know—I wasn't really in the mood—I had been sick for a few days and held out of practice. But when I picked the sticks up, wouldn't you know they all had my name written on the back?"

"That's strange," I agreed.

"Another time, I came in and found a copy of the school paper left open on the floor. It looked like Raven had been using it as a placemat with her crumbs and salt spilled all around it. The paper was a mess! She'd been burning her stupid candles and got red wax all over.

"And you know whose paper it was? *Mine.* I saved it because it had a picture of me after winning the meet against Southern Poly—I was wanting to bring it home to my parents, but it was ruined.

"Raven's such a slob sometimes, and can have such little consideration for others."

But then Jenna offered, good-naturedly, an apology: "I'm sorry. I didn't mean to vent, sir. I guess I'm just nervous, and it's kind of cold out here."

"That's OK," I reassured her. "And you're right—it is getting a little cold. Maybe I had better go and check on those two."

6

The real moon rose, reflecting off the mountaintop and enhancing the effect of a lunar surface. It shone down on the lonely crater where Raven had taken Denilson aside.

I saw two half-empty water bottles and a plastic bag of what appeared to be trail mix nearby and made a mental note to pick them up later.

Raven sat cross-legged across from her lead actor, whispering and staring rather hypnotically into his eyes with what might have passed for romantic interest except for the business at hand.

I had been dubious that the affable athlete could ever get into character. Raven had added some hints of wolf features to his face, but the make-up wasn't doing much to further the lycan illusion. From a distance, the fluff around Denilson's forehead and ears didn't look particularly sinister, although I caught a glint of new teeth that looked razor sharp.

No doubt because the mouthpiece was a bit large, they dripped with real drool.

"It's getting a little late, Raven," I announced quietly. "Jenna's cold and the guys are gone."

"In a minute," she shot back. "We're not quite ready here, yet."

She reached over and stroked Denilson's chest.

I heard a low, guttural growl.

7

"They're taking too long!" Jenna exclaimed. "This really sucks."

I tried my best to reassure her. "That's show biz," I said. "It's always a lot of hurrying up and waiting around."

But Jenna was too overstressed and despondent to reply. I sensed she only wanted to get the ordeal over with.

Finally Raven returned, sans Denilson, and gave me an odd look as if I were suddenly in the way.

At the same time, she seemed unbothered by the desertion of her soccer crew from the set.

"Will you hold this lighting screen?" she asked me.

"Certainly," I replied, albeit wondering how any screen, at this hour, could possibly capture more than a reflection of a reflection of a reflection.

"Places!" Raven snapped, the impersonal command apparently intended for Jenna alone.

Jenna began to protest she had no idea what she was supposed to do, but then Raven stepped over and positioned her manually, with hands on Jenna's shoulders.

The director's eyes were hard and she didn't offer her ingénue actress any further coaching.

Instead, she called out "Ready!" and slid into place behind the camera.

There was a second or two delay.

"Action!" Raven exclaimed, taking both Jenna and I completely off guard.

Like a shot, Denilson appeared over the rise, growling. He tore off his suit with a loud rip, exposing his chest.

But was this Denilson?

The young man's eyes were bloodshot and his smile was replaced with a cruel leer.

Perhaps, I thought, *he could act after all.*

"*Now!*" Raven insisted aloud, despite the fact that we were already rolling. Her voice rose to a husky shriek: "*Now, kill the bitch!*"

Denilson pounced on Jenna, snarling.

Unsure whether she was supposed to recognize anything human in her fellow astronaut and perhaps hold onto that cherished image for a beat or two, Jenna instead reacted quite instinctively to the lycan's approach.

She screamed.

The creature lashed at her, ripping the shoulder of her spacesuit. Viciously, it lunged forward again to bite her neck.

This time Jenna turned and began to run.

And run.

Fortunately for her, she was a good bit more limber than Denilson on the uneven terrain, leaping across rocks while he lunged forward stiffly.

"Y'all get away from me!" she cried.

Jenna fled down the mountain, Denilson gamely loping after her.

I fully expected Raven to yell "cut" at any time. The line of trees leading down the nature trail would clearly constitute a continuity error, given the moon locale.

But Raven appeared to be distracted, and she grew more and more incensed by the progress of the scene.

"*Catch her! Tear her head off!*" she screeched.

As Jenna and Denilson disappeared out of sight, however, the lycan continued to lose ground steadily.

I let the lighting screen drop to the ground.

Raven finally looked over to me with a cruel, far-focused look in her eyes.

She struggled to regain her composure.

"Cut," she said quietly, with a wicked smile.

8

You'll be happy to know Jenna Higgs did, in fact, make it to the bottom of Stone Mountain in one piece.

I called 911 and proceeded to reprimand Raven for the full mile down the mountain trail, telling her I knew she must have drugged Denilson. That she should never have involved others in her little revenge plot on her roommate, that it was just terribly wrong, and she could count herself lucky if no one had gotten killed.

Raven, naturally, tuned me out the entire way.

At the bottom of the trail, it was my turn to face the fire with the police, who had barely been able to get any words out of Jenna.

In the meantime, Denilson was nowhere to be found.

We combed the area for him and continued to do so long afterwards, joined by a growing coterie of soccer players. I had nightmares of the young man either attacking a straggling tourist or perhaps lying dead somewhere in a ravine.

Eventually I saw no point in remaining on site while the search continued to spread, and I offered to drive Jenna back to campus instead.

She was quite dazed and immediately lay down in the back seat and slept.

I later dropped her off in the hands of a campus security guard, telling him not to let Raven Ripley anywhere near her that night.

But the campus was quiet.

As I pulled out of the security gate, the only sign of life I could see was a stray cat. In the semi-darkness, its eyes resembled two glowing holes.

The cat watched me, fixed in the reflection of my headlights for an instant, and then slipped off behind a tree.

9

I needn't have feared—Raven Ripley had carefully planned an exit strategy from the university well in advance.

And I never saw her again. When it came time to turn in fall grades, I gave her an incomplete for her film project that eventually turned into an F. I later heard from another student Raven had headed back north.

The last call I made on that ill-fated night was to Coach Carlson, to inform him his star striker was AWOL and quite possibly out of his mind. I would leave it for him to notify Denilson's family in Brazil.

"I got him right here," Coach replied.

"*What?*"

"He was scratched up pretty bad, but no bones were broken."

Coach Carlson continued: "He's OK now, but doesn't really remember what happened to him, only that he woke up in a barn at the antebellum plantation at Stone Mountain Park. Two of the guys found him there and drove him back.

"Someone really must have messed with the poor kid's brain. When he came to, he was lying nekkid-chested, covered in blood, with a pile of headless chickens nearby.

"He was just in the locker room now, throwing up the heads."

Coach Carlson abruptly shifted his tone with me.

"Kids and their parties! I told him if he ever pulls a stunt like that again, I'll kick his butt off my team."

He paused, just to let this little bit of ham acting sink in.

"So how's he doing in your class, anyway?"

"He'll pass," I said.

LOST IN THE MIX

1

Film festivals aren't quite what they used to be. According to many, the golden era of U.S. independents peaked sometime in the late 1990s, before the subsidiaries began to reclaim lost ground for the studios. Now it's not uncommon for a commercial feature to premiere at a festival to gain a little street cred just weeks before opening in cineplexes.

For this reason, I don't make the rounds of the major festivals as often as I used to. But when I do, I will occasionally see Scott Sliden.

Although he doesn't represent any A-level clients, Scott is a capable guy who worked his way up in the movie industry from assistant director to studio rep to independent agent. If you are a critic, he might casually bump into you after a premiere just to ask how you liked the film, or if you wouldn't mind examining some promotional materials.

I like Scott. But I tend to avoid him at such times, hoping to preserve my unbiased opinions.

Recently, I arrived on the next-to-last day of the Atlanta Film and Video Festival and was less than enthusiastically weighing my options. Clearly, the most talked-about films had already been screened and nominated for awards, and the day's offerings constituted the dregs.

Half-heartedly, I glanced at the afternoon schedule, finding a film called *Vestiges de Plaisir*, a dialogue-heavy piece about a post-sexual Montreal couple struggling to redefine their relationship; and *Tender is the Fright*, an iffy student production featuring two lovelorn teens who spend a night in a haunted house only to end up becoming ghosts themselves.

Faced with such a choice, I was debating whether to turn around to preserve my $12. And so when Scott Sliden approached me in the lobby, sporting a rather posh jacket and an expensive-looking briefcase, I greeted him a little more enthusiastically than usual.

Somewhat taken aback by the warm welcome, Scott stopped in his tracks. He inquired about my daughter.

Not being up to date with Scott's life, I asked him in turn about our mutual acquaintance Victor Tata, a former director of schlock horror pics who had once been Scott's mentor.

"Haven't you heard?" Scott asked, with a look of genuine surprise on his face.

"Victor Tata is dead."

2

I couldn't say I was surprised by Scott's news. I had seen Vic Tata myself only a year prior and the old man had been in pretty sad shape. He relied on his assistant, Manolito Gallo, to help him 24/7.

Even sadder was the impression I received of a man who took no pleasure in his work. Vic had renounced his career and the whole *Hellish* series of films that had once brought him fame (*Hellish Picnic*, *Hellish Job*, *Hellish Afternoon*, and the rest). Late in life, he underwent a religious conversion and, per Scott, had died peacefully in his bed.

"Vic Tata left everything to Manny, of course, which wasn't much."

"The mansion was put up for sale," Scott added, "but there weren't any takers. The place had really fallen from grace since the days Vic used to host those parties à la Hugh Heffner."

Scott, I knew, spoke from experience. Following a nasty divorce, he had moved in with Vic, becoming the director's personal secretary, publicity agent, and—for two years or more—the son he never had.

"Vic named me executor to his estate and left me the rights to all his films. For religious reasons, Manny wasn't interested in collecting any royalties from the *Hellish* series. He went home to Argentina for good and left me the key to the place.

"When I went there to take a look at the books, it was kind of embarrassing. Vic's last few royalty checks weren't even in four figures, unless you count the decimals. The films were old, the special effects cheesy. They had been available on Amazon for eleven years, but almost no one ordered them."

Then one day, over the phone, Manny mentioned something to Scott Sliden about Vic spending several months on a final, never-completed project. This was to be an autobiographical picture, a retrospective look at the early days, and Vic's first serious film. Titled *The Devil's Work*, it told the story of the early successes and the eventual fall from grace in the industry.

The next day, curious, Scott pocketed the key and drove out to the mansion to see if he could find it.

By now the conversation was getting uncomfortably long for the lobby, so I suggested to Scott we walk across the shopping plaza to a Mexican restaurant.

Maybe I was no Wallace Shawn, and this lunch with Scott Sliden wouldn't exactly turn out to be *My Dinner With Andre*—it would, however, afford me a chance to retreat from the festival with dignity.

3

"That first night at the mansion, you know, I thought I *heard* him."

"Heard who?"

"I thought I heard Vic's ghost!"

"You'd better elaborate, Horatio."

Scott took a brief sip from his piña colada and proceeded with his tale.

"I'd been searching the mansion all afternoon, you know, and was tired. So I brushed off a couch in Vic's entertainment room and thought I would crash there for the night and get a fresh start in the morning.

"Besides, it was beginning to storm outside, and I didn't want to drive home in the rain.

"Anyway, I fell asleep.

"I woke up in the middle of the night. It was thundering outside, so I got up to make sure all the windows were secure.

"I watched the rain fall into Vic's old cracked pool for a while. Then as I returned to the couch, I thought I heard a noise—a heartbeat."

"A heartbeat?"

"Yeah, a slow, measured, *ka-thump, ka-thump.*"

Scott continued: "That wasn't all. I also heard a harsher noise of someone whispering *Shhh! Shhh!,* and what sounded like a shudder and creak of a hatch slowly opening.

"A moment later came the murmur of dozens of faraway voices, followed by screams of human beings suffering in horrible pain."

"Wow," I said.

"Finally, a few beats later, Vic's voice sounded out, distinct but muffled, like it was rising up from the earth."

"What was Vic saying?"

"He was moaning, *"Evil . . . evil . . . nothing here but wickedness and evil!"*

"Spooky!"

"I'll say, M.V., I tell you, I couldn't get out of that place fast enough!"

He paused for a moment, taking a deeper sip of his fruity drink.

"But by the next afternoon, of course, I was feeling quite ashamed of my over-reaction. So I drove back and searched that place top to bottom. Nothing."

I asked Scott whether he thought he might have been dreaming the night before.

"Yes. I was really beginning to think so."

"But then it grew dark," he continued, "and the ghostly litany repeated itself: the creaking, the sound of the heartbeat. And finally Vic's voice, rising dramatically, as if from the bottom of an infernal pit: 'Evil . . . evil . . . *nothing here but wickedness and evil!'"*

I had been just about to reach over the table for another tortilla chip, but my hand paused over the basket.

"So what did you do?" I asked, beginning to wonder what I would do myself in such a situation.

Bring in witnesses? Pay them to spend the night to corroborate my story about Vic's unhappy ghost?

"I called in Don Darling," Scott said.

4

I didn't know who Don Darling was at the time but later realized I must have seen his name roll by in film credits many times. He was a sound mixer, and per Scott, one of the best: "He can blend a baby's cry with an eagle's screech and a buzz saw and build you the best ghost you ever heard!"

A sound man.

I had to admit, I liked the idea.

Ghosts have always marked the limits of the acoustical unknown: the echoey stairwell, the drafty chimney flue, the loose tiles on the roof that constitute an Aeolian harp in high winds. Often, ghostly manifestations are simply stand-ins for household problems: torn curtains, smudged windows, cracked pipes, or electrical shorts.

Anyway, with a little persuasion, and a little quid pro quo, Scott got Don Darling to agree to drop by with his equipment in the hope of pinpointing some of the sounds.

5

Don Darling arrived at Vic's mansion and asked Scott to retrace his steps. He followed Scott around the house, leaving a trail of cords and microphones.

Next, he cracked open the sliding glass doors to the pool, went outside, and walked around the deck, shaking his head. The pool was in pretty sad shape, with puddles of water left by the storm and rotting leaves everywhere.

Don, Scott informed me, had actually nailed a couple of noises right away.

Just outside the house, he noticed a dead tree limb that looked like it was about ready to drop off in the pool. He climbed up the tree partway and put all his weight on the branch. It creaked and shuddered just like a door in an old thriller.

"Then Don frowned," Scott continued. "He saw broken boards near the top of the outbuilding housing Vic's sauna. He found a stepladder, climbed up, and peered in. Then he called me over so I could have a look, too.

"Inside, I saw a large nest. 'Barn owl,' Don said. He imitated the sound of the bird's cry for me: '*Shhh! Shhh!*'

"By this time, I was quite impressed by Don's detective skills. True, we still hadn't nailed down the heartbeat, but Don was hot on that scent also, slowly pacing one-foot-in-front-of-the-other from a crack in the concrete toward the house, like a dowser searching for a hidden spring.

"Finally he stopped, pointed to a wall, and asked, 'What's down there?'

"I said I thought it was Vic's rec room—but of course, from that angle, it was impossible to tell.

"Anyway, long story short, it actually turned out to be a small utility closet, where we found a sump pump Don believed must have kicked on during the storm. From upstairs on the couch, it would have sounded just like a heartbeat coming from underground."

Scott now paused his very strange story of ghost-busting—which, to my own untrained ears, had begun to sound rather like a Home Depot fix-it seminar.

We ate our dinner, talking about ourselves for a while, changes to the city of Atlanta, and some mutual acquaintances.

Then we just took a break from talking.

6

After dinner, Scott Sliden resumed his tale.

"Don Darling's next move was calculated to isolate the source of the other sounds. His first transferred all the microphones to the basement from upstairs, where we had already eliminated most ambient noise.

"He took a closer look at the sump pump, then walked back upstairs and out into the garage.

"He opened the fuse box, studied it for a while, and went back downstairs to readjust his microphones.

"By this time, it was getting late. It had started to rain again as it had all week. Whoever said it never rains in Southern California doesn't know about our Februaries!

"Anyway, after about an hour, the pool began to fill, and the leak in the water line caused the basement waterproofing system to kick on. Sure enough, there came the sound of the tell-tale pump: the heartbeat noise.

"For a couple of minutes we heard nothing else. Then Scott's microphones picked up some crisp static and a loud pop.

"Immediately, I heard the somber voice of Victor Tata, coming in just as clearly as if he were sitting at this table: *'Evil . . . evil . . . I see nothing here but wickedness and evil!'*"

Hearing this, Don Darling had jumped out of his chair like a sprinter reacting to a starter's pistol.

He and Scott raced downstairs, tracing the noise from the utility closet through Vic's rec room to a bedroom which had once formed part of a lavish guest suite.

From this point, they followed the sound into a small sitting room, and then, a little further on, to a sealed door.

Just on the other side of the door, the unhappy ghost of Victor Tata spoke again:

"... *wickedness and evil* ... *wickedness and evil* ...."

Without even bothering to search for a key, Don and Scott put their shoulders to the door and burst in.

7

Inside was a small screening room.

A scene from the *Hellish* series played over and over on an endless loop.

Red lights flashed from the screen as devils clawed mercilessly into a crowd of human beings. Screams rose.

Meanwhile, in a cranky and disparaging voice-over, the old director roundly condemned the whole scene.

It was Victor Tata's lost documentary, *The Devil's Work*.

Don later explained to Scott that the waterproofing system and home theater were on the same circuit and the wiring had probably gone bad to boot. When the automatic system started up, it had switched on Vic's AV equipment, too.

Scott drained the remains of his second drink.

"The equipment was not in the best shape, but Don went to work and got the track unstuck. Then we both sat back and watched.

"There was a cut to Vic Tata sitting in an armchair. He launched into a long tirade against the Hollywood studio machine, genre pics catering to the prurient interest of teenage boys, and the lack of moral fiber of popular audiences generally. He sounded, to me, like a less focused version of his old self. A grumpy old man.

"But you know—that kind of rant against Hollywood can go over *big time* with a film festival crowd."

"I've participated in a few of those discussions myself," I admitted.

"Yes, well, it's been received very well," said Scott. "*The Devil's Work* is the consensus favorite for a Grand Jury Prize for Best Documentary Feature here. There's even talk of giving Vic some kind of posthumous directing award."

"What?"

I suddenly realized I had been out of the loop for far, far too long.

8

Scott Sliden noticed my look of utter confusion and took pity.

"I'm sorry if you missed seeing it. But you'll have another chance when all the finalists are screened again next week."

Scott paused before picking up his shiny briefcase.

"Say, M.V.—you're not still a voting member, are you?"

"I'm afraid I've let my membership lapse," I replied, somewhat sheepishly.

"That's okay, that's okay. I've still got a press packet for you," Scott said, generously handing over a stack of materials neatly encased in a colorful binder. On the cover was a bold header:

The Devil's Work: How Hollywood Stole My Soul.

Directed by Victor Tata.

"To be honest," Scott remarked, "the film probably doesn't need much help at this stage. It's already been picked up by a distributor and should be coming soon to a theatre near you."

He then added, a touch more emotion in his voice, "I owe everything to Vic! He left me quite a legacy. Not simply the rights to *Devil's Work*, but to all the other *Hellish* films featured in the documentary, too. There's been quite a revival of interest in them lately."

"You must be a busy man, Scott," I said. "It's a wonder you still have any time for clients."

"Well, I'm not an agent, anymore, really," Scott replied, seeming rather pleased by this fact. "Or at least, I'm free to represent myself now."

"When the phone rings, it rings," he threw in. "Now I can pick it up, or not."

This was definitely a whole new Scott talking. And yes—I realized now that we had just eaten dinner without being interrupted by a single phone call.

Scott Sliden had actually turned his phone *off!*

"Congratulations," I told him, sincerely. "That must be a great feeling."

Scott smiled proudly. But then, like a recovered alcoholic demonstrating he could still hold a bottle, he took the cell phone out of the pocket of his sport coat to scroll through his messages. No doubt, many kudos there.

Absently, I began to pry open a corner of the press packet Scott had handed me.

Out popped a postcard-sized theatre bill.

On it was a still shot, taken from the movie, of Vic leaning forward on his armchair with a sour expression on his face.

It looked like he had just caught some teenagers cutting across his lawn and was about to give them the lecture of their lives.

I smiled.

Rest in peace, Vic.

TROUBLE IN PARADISE VALLEY

1

"Have you ever seen a Chinchorro mummy?" Hap Udall asked me.

"They're really quite beautiful," he commented, "the product of an aesthetic process of transfiguration. Some bodies were dismembered and the limbs reattached with ash paste, as though the artist wished to refashion a new human being using better, longer-lasting materials. Other bodies were hollowed and filled with dried grass or animal hair. The skin was removed and tanned like leather, then painted a resplendent black manganese or red ochre. The face was covered with a clay mask, disk-shaped and marked with delicate holes or a neat slit to suggest a mouth; as the mummies wear smooth over time, the effect is rather like the stylized head of a Cycladic figurine."

This speech would have been quite a mouthful for anyone but Hap, who was a former student of mine.

I had often noticed there seemed to be a kind of inverse ratio between Hap's conversation and the banality of the writing project he was currently assigned to work on, which in this case was pretty mediocre indeed: a shooting script called *Spring Break Planet*. You couldn't blame Hap for that, though. As Dr. Johnson said, "No man but a blockhead ever wrote, except for money."

"The Chinchorro Mummies of Peru?"

"That's right," Hap said. "Did you know the Chinchorro burial tradition stretches back as far as 7000 A.D.? That's thousands of years before Egypt."

"Interesting," I said.

"Of course, the oldest mummies found in the region are natural ones, desiccated bodies preserved by the desert heat. They were slow to decompose, and had a way of popping out of hillsides and shallow graves."

"Yes," I replied, looking out at the crest of the mountain just above us. "Occasionally that kind of thing happens around here."

I watched as a lazy cloud drifted over the mountain.

"It was only when the climate became wetter and bodies began to decompose faster that the Chinchorro began to perfect their own techniques."

The cloud looked somewhat out of place in the otherwise clear sky.

2

Hap and I sat out on the deck of my friend Gideon Smith's rental property in Paradise Valley, Arizona, overlooking a place called Mummy Mountain. The name of the place had, naturally, suggested our topic of conversation.

There are Mummy Mountains in a lot of states, mountain ranges which readily suggest to the eye the outline of an Egyptian sarcophagus.

I'm not a fan of the name, with its suggestion of Luxor in America. Personally, I would have preferred the original designation, Windy Gap, or perhaps the Hohokam name for the place, if anyone still remembered it.

This Mummy Mountain might have been beautiful, had it not been built up so heavily, or if every turn of the trail hadn't revealed a view of Scottsdale.

But I had made my peace with it that morning, having located a nearby path and done a little hiking to the top. There I had found a little community of cacti and a creosote bush. I suddenly felt nostalgic for that musky, rainy smell creosote has when it gets wet.

Later I rested on a rock and watched the sun come up over a nearby peak, just as the Hohokam skywatchers had done many centuries ago.

3

Gideon joined us with glasses of sun tea from the kitchen. None of us drank anything more potent than that: Hap was a Mormon, I was a lightweight, and Gideon had been sober for over twenty-five years.

He had been my roommate in film school at the University of Arizona. I had just flown out to visit him at the end of June so we could drive down to Tucson together for our thirtieth class reunion.

For me, the trip was really more of an excuse to decompress from another semester of teaching and take refuge in the desert. After my hike that morning, I was more eager than ever to get out of town.

Gideon was the brains behind *Spring Break Planet.*

As a producer, he had brought in Hap to do a little last-minute script doctoring on the project, nothing major. Hap had flown down from Utah.

I didn't ask, and didn't want to know, how such a film merited a rewrite; and Hap, of course, would rather talk about practically anything else.

And anyway, he was finished. He had stayed up to complete the job in one night, and now Gideon and I were going to drop him off at the airport on our way to the set.

4

Gideon Smith circulated among the film crew, handing out Hap's new orange-colored script pages and instructing everyone to replace the beige-colored pages in their copies with those.

I wandered over the set, which featured enormous speakers and a light stage. *Spring Break Planet* was an expensive production starring the popular singing group The ABC Crunk Girls: Alesa, Baby, and Carmen. It was the often-difficult Alesa, Gideon informed me, who had demanded the rewrite.

A gleaming spaceship stood on a small rise at the edge of a barren wash. The wash was supposed to stand in for the surface of the alien planet, where the Crunk Girls land on their mission to spread partying throughout the universe.

Over one hundred young dancers, dressed in green costumes with retro Martian-looking antennae, were doing some last-minute rehearsing.

They were instructed to encircle the ship and make some Caliban-like threatening noises and gestures until the hatch of the craft opened and the Girls descended in a haze of pink mist and jousting laser-lights.

Captain Alesa would first greet the home crowd aliens with a little speech, and then give a dramatic command to the sweet-natured Baby to train the party-ray on them in order to get things started. Next, the balletic Carmen would do a series of hand springs down the ramp before flinging herself into the crowd of cheering space-lings in order to teach them how to really get down.

That sort of thing.

Standing near the small hill supporting the spacecraft were dozens of sound and light crew members tinkering with last-minute adjustments.

Above the hill, a few more clouds had gathered, but it looked like it was going to remain a clear afternoon for filming.

It was a busy set—and, for the most part, a pleasant one.

Just off to one side of the spacecraft, however, I noticed a young man who seemed distinctly out of place.

This man, who appeared to be college or graduate-school age, wore a wide-brimmed hat, tan vest, and fatigues. On his back was a large pack with some kind of plastic sheeting sticking out of it and pouches for digging tools and a canteen.

He was not looking too happy. I thought I might do Gideon a favor by seeing what the matter was.

"Do you know who's in charge here?" the young man asked me.

"Maybe," I said. "But this is a closed set. Are you sure you're supposed to be here?"

"It's a state park!" he exclaimed, exasperated.

"True. But this film crew has been granted special authorization to be here, for a considerable fee. That money helps the park with its operating expenses."

"Hah!" he said. "You can bet whatever money the State of Arizona collects is going to be diverted toward some conservative cause, or some big-wig's pet development project."

"I don't know," I said, finding myself oddly sympathizing with him. "Are you with the Occupy movement, or something?"

"No, I'm an anthropologist," he replied. "A graduate student at ASU."

He continued: "Do you know that glyphs have been found on some of the rocks nearby?"

I told him that I didn't.

"They might date back to Sacaton Phase!" the young man said. "There are signs of pit houses, and those idiots may have parked their spaceship on an ancient platform mound."

"A burial site?" I asked.

"Inhumation was not unknown among the Hohokam," the anthropologist lectured, "although cremation was more common. More than likely, this could have been a religious site of some kind."

I looked at the heavy metal spaceship, which had sunk into the sandy soil at the top of the rise. In order to offset this, and to preserve the dramatic look of an alien cliff, the crew had dug trenches all around the sides of the mound, making it appear much larger and steeper.

As they continued to adjust cables around smaller pits that housed laser projectors, dust crumbled down.

"It's desecration!" the graduate archaeologist said. "They've got to stop this now! I'll . . . I'll call the police! Or the news station!"

"Just hold on a minute," I told him. "I'll let you talk to someone."

5

Gideon, as I knew, was pretty good at handling this sort of thing.

Ordinarily I would have approached one of the assistant directors first, but I didn't want to listen to my old friend complain all the way to Tucson that I had let some weird guy get away to create bad PR for the film, whether or not any ABC Crunk Girl fans really cared.

Gideon had brought a security guard with him, just in case.

"I want to reassure you, Mr.—"

"My name's not important."

"—Yes, well, Mr. Whoever you are, that we are not setting out to desecrate anything or offend anyone. This is an innocent little movie, and we are going to be packed up and out of here in two days."

"In the meantime, I suppose your dancers are going to trample all around that platform mound?"

"What platform mound?" Gideon snapped, starting to lose a little patience. "We built that mound up ourselves, for the shoot. You are assuming this is some well-established archaeological site; and that, sir, is not a fact. You are only speculating."

"Of course I'm *hypothesizing*," the young man retorted, not backing down. "What do you know about archaeology?"

"I have nothing but respect for archaeology," Gideon replied, more gently. "As does my colleague Dr. Montgomery, who first brought your concern to my attention.

"But from a logistical standpoint, you'll have to agree filming the mound today is already a fait accompli. We could have made a change to our shooting schedule earlier, and I wish you had stepped forward then. It's my job to make those kinds of adjustments and to try to keep all parties happy."

If he had known more, I don't think the young man would have felt very reassured by the fact that Gideon's recent duties included giving Alesa Crunk a longer speech and more face time on camera.

"I know you're upset, and perhaps have every right to be," Gideon continued, "but we have promised park officials we will leave the desert wash just as we found it, and take nothing."

The young man remained impassive.

"I tell you what—maybe we can put in a good word for you. Say we have reason to suspect we might have disturbed a possible Indian burial mound and know an archaeologist who would like to keep the area roped off for a while.

"Perhaps we can even throw a little more money Bill Hilson's way, as a donation. Let me talk to Bill first, but I think I can make that happen for you: a dig site with a rope line only *you* can cross."

The offer of being put in charge of a dig must have been an attractive one to any graduate student looking for an opportunity. And in fact, the young man began to look to me uncertainly just as Gideon's phone rang.

"Excuse me a minute," Gideon said. "I have to take this."

While he had a chance, the young man approached me and asked, "Is this guy giving me the runaround? Can he really do that?"

"Believe me, it's a simple phone call for him," I said, "and just a little more grease to the wheel of the park board.

"Honestly, you know, he doesn't have to do any of this. The scene is going to be shot. Going to the press wouldn't stop a thing; perhaps only generate a little publicity for the film, which most studios would consider a boon.

"But Mr. Smith's trying to close this picture today," I concluded. "So you're lucky—you caught him at just the right time."

The producer returned, handed the student a card and said, "Gotta go."

"Baby Crunk is feeling a little overheated," he added by way of apology, "and I've got to go hold her hand for a while."

"Baby Crunk of the ABC Crunk Girls?" the young man asked, somewhat bashfully.

Of the Crunk Girls, Baby is variously referred to as the middle one, the black one, or the sweet one. She's a quite striking former swimsuit model.

"That's right," Gideon replied. "Want to meet her?"

6

Late that afternoon, Gideon and I finally managed to steal away from the set in his rental car.

He was not the film's line producer, but one of several behind-the-scenes executives who had gotten the production off the ground in the first place. He would never have stuck around this long during the shooting if it hadn't been for a few snafus such as the rewrite.

We had only driven as far as Casa Grande, however, when the big drops began to explode against the windshield.

Gideon's initial reaction was denial. He recalled the mostly clear skies we had left behind in Phoenix and remarked, "Probably nothing to worry about."

But Gideon hadn't lived in Arizona for many years and had forgotten something important. In the desert, there were five annual seasons, not four. Fall, winter, spring, dry summer, and of course . . .

. . . monsoon season.

When he finally pulled the car over to check his messages, he found half a dozen urgent texts, all of them sent within the last two minutes.

Gideon cursed and gave me a look that meant sorry, fun's over.

7

When we returned, the set was in an advanced state of chaos.

The wash now appeared to house a small river, which the film crew did its best to block and divert.

Several crew members tried to create a little room for run-off by digging trenches near the edge of the arroyo, but there was no place for that much water to go.

Their party over, the alien dancers had dispersed to their trailers, while the ABC Crunk Girls retreated into the safest place available, the spaceship on the high knoll.

There, they sullenly waited and watched the flash flood through the bubble of their craft. The hatch was firmly closed, but the waters continued to build below.

Noticing this, I warned Gideon that the mound was probably not the safest place in the world for anyone to be. The sides had been dug out, and as the flood waters rose, large sections of dried earth were flaking off.

"Get the talent off that hill," Gideon shouted into his cell phone. "It looks like it could go any minute."

But this warning came too late.

With a sudden burst, the flash flood breached the film crew's improvised barriers. Suddenly soaked on all sides, the mound started to sag in the middle like dough. The spaceship tilted forward and then slid down the mud embankment into the wash.

Its pointed prow jabbed into the ground, and the cupola popped open.

8

I heard the ABC Crunk Girls scream in unison like hatchlings in a fallen nest. They didn't appear to be in any immediate danger, but the situation was certainly a scary one and they were getting soaked.

Then, predictably, things got even worse.

Relieved of its burden, the top of the hill quickly became saturated.

Mud washed down on the faux spaceship, splattering the Girls and threatening a landslide.

More shrieks.

But it was much too risky, at the moment, for any rescuers to approach.

Some rocks and rubble dislodged and started to cascade down the hill, ricocheting off the stern of the ship.

Throughout, the set remained brightly lit. It might have been my imagination, but I thought I caught a flash or two of color. I had to wonder if some objects pelting the ship might have been stone figures or ceramics.

Then the rest of the mound collapsed, and I saw something else:

Bodies.

Lots of them, perhaps as many as eight or nine. Adult-sized, and much smaller. Partially wrapped, and unwrapped.

It was raining mummies.

Alesa Crunk and Carmen Crunk did their best to dodge the bodies, Carmen rising and kicking at them to defend the cockpit.

But Baby Crunk had reached the breaking point and wanted out. She panicked and climbed out of her seat. Then she slid down the nose cone of the plane, right above the raging torrent.

"Somebody help her!" I heard several people yell in unison.

One of those voices might have been Gideon's. In the pouring rain, it was impossible to tell who was standing nearby.

By contrast, the whole area of the wash was still lit up like noon. So we all watched helplessly as Baby Crunk, clinging to the spaceship's faux fuselage, slowly lost her grip and plunged into the water.

The current spun her around once in a complete circle, and then she went under.

9

Almost immediately, I heard a pained yelp from back at the mound area.

I turned to see a young man appear out of nowhere, surfing down the mudslide and landing hard against the hull of the spaceship.

He raced along the top of the craft toward the cockpit, brushing aside a couple of mummies. Without missing a beat, he dove off the prow heroically in the area where Baby Crunk had disappeared.

Just before he splashed into the water, I caught a look of determination in the young man's face and recognized him.

Who else but our graduate anthropologist would be reckless enough to jump in?

In stunned silence, we all watched as the man resurfaced, spat out some water, dogpaddled out a little further, and submerged again.

The tension around the set rose. For several seconds, there was nothing to see but a small eddy in the current where the man had gone down.

Then, simultaneously, fortuitously, two heads emerged from the water.

One belonged to a former supermodel, covered in mud but sputtering and clearly alive. The other belonged to a grad student who still sported a look of concern.

We applauded.

The young man struggled to get Baby Crunk to higher ground where he could stand. Tenderly cradling her in one arm, he thrashed and fought against the current until he finally found a foothold.

As we shouted out our encouragement, he picked up Baby in a fireman's carry. Laboriously, he waded toward the side of the wash.

Several crew members splashed out to meet him.

Somewhat reluctantly, the young man handed Baby Crunk over to them.

We applauded again.

10

The film crew attached a winch to the Crunk Spacecraft and hauled it to the side of the wash, where the two remaining stars were helped out and escorted to their trailer.

The monsoon had let up, long enough for me to make out the solitary figure of Gideon standing nearby. He was silhouetted in a corona of rain and background lighting.

I suddenly felt sorry for my old friend. Putting my hand on his shoulder, I said, "I'm sorry, Gideon. I know this little disaster is going to cost you plenty."

I added: "But at least no one was hurt."

Gideon said nothing for a minute, continuing to stare onto the scene of destruction below.

Then he turned to me, and I could see he had a grin on his face.

"Good to know you're OK, too."

"You don't look too upset," I said.

"Let me show you something," he replied, gesturing me over.

I peered down into the wash, saw Baby Crunk, now wrapped in a large beach blanket, skipping back over to the graduate anthropologist. She bent down, lifted his face to hers, and they kissed. Behind them, the gleaming spaceship looked like it had just crash-landed on the earth; and the rough water, illuminated by balloon lights, created a surreal landscape which was, admittedly, mesmerizing.

"It's kind of beautiful," I remarked.

"Not the set, you silly poet. Look over *there*," Gideon said, pointing toward the far embankment.

I followed a different angle and saw what appeared to be a small second camera set up beside the bank of the wash.

The four crew members appeared to be celebrating and high-fiving.

"They've been rolling the whole time, working on a little project I prearranged called "The Making of *Spring Break Planet*," Gideon said.

"It was going to be a special feature on the DVD," he added. "But now, I don't know," he said, looking thoughtful.

"That would be one hell of a special feature," I said. You've got a disaster, a rescue, and even a kind of classic romance unfolding between the nerdy scientist and the beautiful but modest sex symbol."

I was now thinking out loud, too: "Not to mention mummies."

We both stood there a long time without talking.

Special feature, huh.

Or maybe with another rewrite, a whole other movie?

Gideon finally asked me, "Are you thinking what I'm thinking?"

"Yes," I replied. "You had better give Hap Udall another call."

ACKNOWLEDGMENTS

My thanks to the editors of *Devilfish Review, The Northville Review, Prospective, Penduline Press, Roadside Fiction, Sorcerous Signals, Static Movement,* and *Z-composition,* in which several of these pieces previously appeared.

Special thanks to Sarah McDonald of *Devilfish* for her assistance with the story "Clickerland," to Ash Hartwell for his advice regarding the stories "The Heart of the Matter" and "A Methodical Madness," and to Jessica Kristie of Winter Goose Publishing for her suggestions on the development of this book.

I am also grateful to the Office of Sponsored Research and Scholarly Activity at Life University (OSRSA) for its support of creative work.

Thanks to my sister Molly, who previewed most of the stories in their original form, and to the rest of my family.

Finally, thanks to Alfred Hitchcock, my favorite comedian.

ABOUT THE AUTHOR

M.V. Montgomery is an English and film professor at Life University in Marietta, Georgia. He is the author of three previous collections of fiction: *Dream Koans*, *Antigravitas*, and *Circle, Triangle, Square*.

Follow M.V. Montgomery on his website:
mvmontgomery.wordpress.com

FICTION by M.V. Montgomery

DREAM KOANS

"*Dream Koans*, which consists of various themes and statements, leaves the reader in awe of M.V. Montgomery's imagination. As an eclectic collection, it does not read so differently than Gertrude Stein's *Tender Buttons*, and this is clearly its success. The flash fiction ranges from exaggerated melodramatic scenes to ridiculous impossibilities from unheard-of creatures. And the multitude of characters—family, famous people, academics and animals–evokes an independent world."

—Dustin Dill, *Fast Forward Press*

"M.V. Montgomery has distilled the narrative concept down to an incredibly pure form, one which does nothing but enhance the humor, subtlety, and emotional weight of these dreamlike vignettes."

—Robert Lieberman, *Conte Online*

"M.V. Montgomery's stories don't preach about how to write yet raise questions about what writing means and how it can happen."

—William Males, *Frostwriting*

"Creativity explodes from this . . . and a lesson can be learned by all writers drudging through the same stagnant form again and again, myself included. I'm going to think of M.V. Montgomery the next time I begin crafting in that same tired pattern: *Action, Background, Development, Climax, Ending*. Greatness comes from breaking form. I'm learning. Thanks, M.V."

—Daniel McDermott, *Bananafish*

ANTIGRAVITAS

"*Antigravitas* is an interesting and very vivid collection of flash fiction, muses, and short stories that are as odd and quirky as they are funny and unique—and if you share in having a wry and dark sense of humor, then many of these writings will definitely resonate with you."

—Cinsearae S., *Dark Gothic Resurrected*

"M. V. Montgomery is a twenty-first century Borges—a comparison I don't make lightly. His vivid images and open, powerful language will follow you off the page. With surprise encounters with zombies, Mark Twain, extended family and the people across the street, Antigravitas speaks to everything from self-judgment to the creative process."

—Megan Arkenberg, *Mirror Dance*

"After reading M.V. Montgomery's new collection, I shared it immediately with a friend. I couldn't keep it a secret. For days my friend and I discussed. We couldn't decide whether or not these stories were to be taken for dreams or reality. There are ghosts, certainly. And human clones, and tumbleweed entities. But what humanity there is behind these imaginings! What surprising vulnerability from the consciousness of this storyteller.

"In the end, my friend and I decided it matters not what can and does happen in this book, but merely that it happens for the reader, that it happened for the writer. For when you encounter these sentences, you come to know Montgomery himself, and the experience is haunting."

—Nicholas Maistros, *Palooka*